The Bill

ABOUT THE AUTHOR

Tony Lynch works as a feature writer specialising in television, films, photography and sport. He is the author of "Dickens's England – A Travellers' Companion", and co-author of "Striker" with Gary Lineker and "The Fincher File" with Terry Fincher.

The Bill

THE INSIDE STORY OF BRITISH TELEVISION'S MOST SUCCESSFUL POLICE SERIES

Tony Lynch

B⬚XTREE

THAMES
TELEVISION

ACKNOWLEDGEMENTS

The author would like to thank the following for their help in the preparation of this book: The cast of *The Bill*; Geoff McQueen; Executive Producer Michael Chapman; former Executive Producer Peter Cregeen; Casting Director Pat O'Connell; Booking Assistant Harriet Kimmel; photographer Stan Allen; Police Advisor Brian Hart; Property Master Dave Hodges; Archivist Ruth Parkhill; Simon Crook of Action Vehicles; Sara Drake of Thames International; Jan Daniels and Dianne Strachan of *Sierra Oscar*; Jim Maloney for compiling The Story So Far ... Boxtree Senior Editor Rod Green and in particular Unit Publicist Wendy Tayler and Project Co-ordinator Nigel Wilson who together opened the doors of Sun Hill and brought the cast members in for questioning.

First published in the UK in 1991
by BOXTREE LIMITED, 36 Tavistock Street,
London WC2E 7PB

12345678910

Design and computer page make up by Penny Mills
Cover design by Paterson Jones
Photographs by Stan Allen, Tony Lynch, John Paul, Laurie Asprey, and Pat Dyos
Picture Research by Wendy Tayler, Rod Green and Tony Lynch

Printed and bound in bound in Great Britain by Butler and Tanner Limited, Frome, Somerset

A catalogue record for this book is available from the British Library

ISBN – 1 85283 157 X

Introduction

In a magazine review of police drama series on television, in March 1991, John Stalker declared Thames TV's *The Bill* to be '...in a class of its own [giving] an accurate view of what modern policemen do – one minute they're fending off mad dogs, the next they're dealing with lost children. What it loses in car chases, it gains in accurate detail, right down to the relationships between officers, and all the paperwork. It's by far and away the best'.

That's praise indeed from the high profile ex-Deputy Chief Constable of Greater Manchester.

A number of other real policemen list the programme among their favourite viewing. One constable, taking a break from crowd control duty outside Wembley Stadium in April 1991, confirmed to the author of this book that he and his professional colleagues watch *The Bill* whenever they can and are consistently impressed by its attention to detail and the unerring accuracy displayed – especially in relation to the never-ending reams of paperwork. "The forms they fill in are spot-on," he said. He also added, in a somewhat resigned tone, that there was "a whinger just like Reg Hollis, down at our station".

John Stalker's sentiments are vehemently echoed by the millions of British viewers who tune in regularly, at 8 o'clock each Tuesday and Thursday evening, to catch up with the latest happenings down at the Sun Hill police station. *The Bill* is also a top rated show in Australia and New Zealand – and the series has been sold to more than twenty five other countries from Sweden to Swaziland.

The Bill is the most successful police drama series in the history of British television. This book tells the story behind that success.

1 From *Woodentop* to *The Bill*

G eoff McQueen could be described as the archetypal late-developer – at least as far as creative writing is concerned. "I was 29 years old when I sat down to read a book for the first time in my life," admits the devisor of *The Bill*. "One of my sisters had often told me that I'd enjoy reading, but somehow I just hadn't got round to it. Then came a period when I was working abroad a lot, living out of suitcases in various hotels, and I found myself with lots of time on my hands. I was getting very bored, so I decided to see what was so special about this reading business. I bought a paperback and settled down to read it..."

The book he chose was Alistair MacLean's *HMS Ulysses*, a rollicking good yarn about the crew and the travels of an Arctic convoy ship in World War Two. Maclean's snappy style and the relentless drive of the narrative make the book a real page turner.

"I was knocked out by it," said Geoff. "It was tremendous stuff, a terrific story. From then on I was hardly ever bored in my spare time – I was hooked on books. It was as if a new world had opened up for me. And I was probably making up for lost time, because over the next two years I read around six novels a week, mainly thrillers."

In time this late-comer to books began to harbour ambitions to become a writer. "I was forever coming up with story ideas of my own – I knew I had to make a decision about my future. I wanted to write, but had no idea of how to go about it. And I was hopeless at spelling."

By then Geoff and his wife Jan and their two sons Matthew and Greg were living in Royston, Hertfordshire, where McQueen worked as general manager of an electronics company specialising in sound equipment.

One evening, as his son Greg and a young friend were building a Lego castle on the living room carpet, McQueen Snr found himself attempting to compose a rather delicate letter to the tax authorities. Beside him lay a dictionary, with which he would later check the spelling of any suspect words.

As the boys' castle grew, they ran out of bricks and began bickering with one another. "I knew there was another box of Lego in the garden shed, but I didn't want to fetch it because I was concentrating on the letter and having the usual inner argument with myself. Really, I was getting more and more frustrated with myself. I lost my temper with the boys, then stormed out to the shed to get their Lego. As I carried the box back inside, it suddenly dawned on me that I had no excuses whatsoever for not writing, because all my 'Lego' – all my building blocks, all my words – were right there in the dictionary. I would simply have to write my story and then go through it carefully correcting the spelling."

Having made the decision that would eventually change his life, Geoff McQueen resigned from his safe and secure job. A year later he had completed a novel entitled *Time Factor*, a thriller written between part-time jobs. He sent the manuscript off to the various publishers of his favourite thrillers. And one-by-one they each rejected his first literary effort. "It·was a good story, badly written, a typical first novel. But the experience was well worthwhile and taught me a great deal about myself as a writer. I knew, for instance, that my main strength was the creation of believable dialogue. Whenever I got to a dialogue sequence in the book, the thing just flowed along. I realised I have a natural ear for the way people speak to one another."

It was a hard-learned lesson that McQueen would later put to good use. Meanwhile, however, the family were in dire financial straits. "We were even on first-name terms with the bailiff – but somehow I always managed to pay the bills."

While browsing one day in Royston's Manor Bookshop, he picked up a copy of Malcolm Hulke's *Writing For Television* in the '70s – a complete guide to the art of TV script-writing. "I was down to my last fiver, which wasn't enough to buy the book. But the manager, God bless him, said I could pay the balance later."

That evening McQueen read the book from cover-to-cover and as he turned the pages it became apparent that writing for television wasn't very far removed from the kind of writing he had done in the better passages of his failed thriller. The book also pointed out that believable dialogue is an essential ingredient of successful television writing. "I had no idea of the proper form or length of a TV script, but the book had familiarised me with the way a script is laid out – so I decided to have a go."

After much trial and error he came up with a one-off police drama entitled *Till His Eyes Watered* which contained a particularly ingenious ending – involving murder by toilet paper impregnated with *bacillus botulinus* (botulism), a literal twist in the tail. He posted a copy of the script to the BBC Script Unit at TV Centre, and then returned to his part-time work.

Two months later he received a glowing response from Jack Henderson, the Head of the Script Unit. Even though the script was far too long in television terms, Henderson was nevertheless bowled over by the quality of its dialogue. He also added that in his experience of forty years of script reading he thought he knew every method of dispatching a victim. Yet McQueen's ghastly, almost unthinkable, method had managed to make even this seasoned professional squirm in his seat.

Henderson felt that the story would fit well in an established police

Police Hierarchy

Commissioner
Deputy Commissioner
Assistant Commissioners
Deputy Assistant
Commissioners
Commanders
Chief Superintendents
Superintendents
Chief Inspectors
Inspectors
Sergeants
Constables

The Bill's opening titles sequence consists of specially staged scenes and clips from past epsiodes – and is revised from time to time to reflect any cast changes.

The titles always carry *The Bill*'s distinctive logo – the constable's profile in silhouette, above a typewriter-style typeface – and always includes a 'programme devisor' credit to Geoff McQueen, plus the episode title and the names of the Scriptwriter and Director.

Approximately 25 minutes later the closing credits roll over one of *The Bill*'s most distinctive images – the shot of

two police officers' feet walking away from the camera along a rain-soaked cobbled street.

There have been three versions of this shot, the most recent being produced to increase the speed of the closing sequence (in order to make a few more precious seconds available for commercials). Actress Karen England has put her best foot forward as the female officer in all three versions, while the size nines of the current male officer belong to Paul Page-Hanson who has appeared twice.

Topping and tailing the programme is the equally distinctive 'Overdrive', *The Bill*'s staccato theme tune, which was specially composed for the show by Andy Pask and Charlie Morgan.

series which, he explained, was the best route for a promising writer to take into the business. The only BBC police drama running at that time was *Juliet Bravo*, starring Anna Carteret, which was obviously too rural for McQueen's city-based story. Jack Henderson was nevertheless convinced that the author of *Till His Eyes Watered* should be encouraged and he concluded his letter with the news that he had forwarded the script to Michael Verney-Elliot, producer of *The Gentle Touch* at London Weekend Television.

"I was invited down to LWT to meet Michael on the following Monday morning," recalls McQueen. "But I later had to re-arrange the meeting for the Tuesday, because that was the day our Family Allowance came in and therefore the only day I could afford the train fare to London."

Michael Verney-Elliot decided that *Till His Eyes Watered* wasn't suited to *The Gentle Touch* either – but he asked Geoff to come up with the synopsis of a storyline for a *Gentle Touch* episode within the next two weeks. It wasn't a firm commission, just an exploratory exercise to see if McQueen could in fact meet a deadline with an original story. "I wasn't familiar with proper TV scripts, in fact I'd never seen one before so they gave me four *Gentle Touch* scripts to study. That same evening I sat down to write it up as a synopsis – which I now know is one of the hardest things for a writer to do – and about a third of the way through I got fed up and yanked it out of the typewriter, screwed it up and threw it in the rubbish bin."

Over the next four days, judging scene lengths from the scripts he had been given, Geoff McQueen wrote the complete script. He entitled the script *Be Lucky Uncle* and sent it off to *The Gentle Touch* offices at LWT. "I'll never forget Michael Verney-Elliot's reaction. He called immediately to remind me that he hadn't commissioned a complete script from me. I explained that I'd got fed up with poncing around with trying to write it as a synopsis and had decided to write the whole thing instead. Then I asked him what he thought of it – and, thankfully, he said he loved it."

Eventually Verney-Elliott did commission the script and *Be Lucky Uncle*, directed by Gerry Mill, was first broadcast in October 1982, giving Geoff McQueen his first screen credit. By then the new TV scriptwriter had teamed-up with an agent, Penny Tackaberry of the Tessa Sayle Agency, the woman who would help to guide him to the very top echelons of his chosen profession, although to Geoff it seemed a long, slow climb. "For more than a year I sent in ideas for single TV plays, but I didn't seem to be getting anywhere. Meanwhile, I was still in deep financial trouble and was by now working part-time in a metalwork factory. Then Penny suggested that I should try to think up some ideas for potential series. Next day I wrote three different treatments *The Maynard File, Cue For The Top* and *Old Bill* and sent them off to her."

Penny Tackaberry was delighted with the package. She felt that each of these ideas would be strong enough to interest the BBC and subsequently presented them to David Reed, then Head of Series at Television Centre. A few days later she called with the news that Reed particularly liked one of the treatments and now wanted to meet the writer. "David preferred *Cue For The Top*, a seven episode drama set in the world of London's snooker halls, places I knew only too well from my own mis-spent youth."

This proved to be the big break that Geoff McQueen had been waiting for. *Cue For The Top* was eventually made by the BBC as *Give Us A Break*, produced by Terry Williams and starring Robert Lindsay and Paul McGann. McQueen was involved at every stage in the production. "I was in my element, at last. I'd found my niche."

Give Us A Break became a huge popular success, commanding a regular spot in the all-important ratings – building from an initial 8,000,000 viewers per episode to around 11,000,000 by the time the series closed. This success also had the practical effect of restoring McQueen's financial status to his bank manager's liking, a situation that was further improved when the BBC commissioned a second – ten episode – series of *Give Us A Break*.

McQueen had written two of the new episodes when the entire project was suddenly scrapped because Robert Lindsay was unavailable: he was committed to a Shakespearean role at the Royal Exchange Theatre in Manchester and was due to follow that immediately with the lead in the London production *Me and My Girl*, which of course became an enormous hit and eventually took Lindsay to the bright lights of Broadway. "Naturally, I was very disappointed, but there was nothing to be done about it – Bob was irreplaceable."

Meanwhile, Terry Williams was left with ten 50-minute segments of screen time to fill. He asked Geoff McQueen to apply his fertile mind

Trudie Goodwin and Mark Wingett in *Woodentop*. WPC Ackland "puppy-walked" the rookie PC Jimmy Carver.

to the problem. "That evening I hit the typewriter and worked through the night to create the basic structure of *Big Deal*, which centred on the gambler Bobby Box."

The new idea was quickly accepted by Terry Williams and, as Geoff set to work on a new batch of scripts, the show was cast with Ray Brooks as Bobby Box and Sharon Duce as his long-suffering girlfriend, Jan. *Big Deal* went on to enjoy even greater success than *Give Us A Break* – with an average weekly audience of 12,000,000 it ran for three series with other writers also contributing scripts.

In a relatively short space of time Geoff McQueen had established the kind of superstar status for which many television writers would give their eye-teeth. It seemed he had a kind of Midas Touch and knew almost instinctively what would work in terms of small screen drama. His reputation went before him and led to an invitation from producer Michael Chapman of Thames TV for McQueen to submit an idea for *Storyboard*, an experimental series specifically created to try out several different ideas, each with 'regular series' potential. Geoff resurrected *Old Bill*, one of the original series ideas presented to the BBC, which had now evolved in his mind into a trilogy of plays – each dealing with a different rank in the police force. Michael Chapman liked the basic premise and asked him to condense it into a single script.

The result was a play about the first day on the beat of probationary constable Jimmy Carver, a liberal-minded young man and an admirer of 'old fashioned policing methods'. It turned out to be an eventful day for the rookie Carver. Together with WPC Ackland he discovered the decomposing body of an old lady in a bath. And he later ran the risk of

Geoff McQueen is a tough, wiry-looking character who could convincingly portray a seen-it-all sergeant or even some hardened miscreant in *The Bill*.

He was born in Dalston, East London in 1947, the fifth child in a family of eleven children. As a boy he was not academically minded and admits to having spent most of his 'schooldays' either running the streets with his mates, or helping his father in the building trade.

However, he was good at football and was taken on as a youth by West Ham United in 1965. But, like many hopeful youngsters before and after him, Geoff had to suffer the disappointment of being told by the club that, in their opinion, he would never make the grade as a professional player. The 'Hammers' released him after almost a year and he became an apprentice carpenter/joiner.

In September 1967, at the age of twenty, he married his childhood sweetheart, Jan Reeve. Their first son, Matthew, was born in 1968. A few months later the young family emigrated to Sydney where Geoff worked as a carpenter and supplemented his income by playing semi-professional football for the Melita Eagles, who played in the New South Wales Premier Division.

The family returned to England after three

years and settled in a small flat in south Tottenham. Geoff worked as a designer and builder of 'English' pubs which were exported to various Continental holiday resorts. The job called for a great deal of travelling. "I would usually work on a

site from seven in the morning to seven at night. Then it was back to the hotel for a quick wash, a change of gear and a bit of nosh before hitting the nightclubs. After a few months of that, you soon get bored. It was this lifestyle that set me on the road to writing when I bought Alistair Maclean's book."

A second son, Greg, arrived in 1971 and the McQueens settled in Royston, Hertfordshire. And it was here that McQueen's writing ambitions would eventually flourish.

Since his successes with *Give Us A Break*, *Big Deal* and *The Bill*, Geoff has penned the comedy series *Home James*, starring Jim Davidson, the comedy-drama *Stay Lucky*, with Dennis Waterman and Jan Francis, a one-off episode of *Lovejoy* for his good friend Ian McShane, and an adaptation of the Dick Francis thriller *Twice Shy* which also starred McShane.

Geoff McQueen rarely contributes epsiodes of *The Bill* these days, and no longer creates new Sun Hill characters. "I think 'Tosh' Lines was one of the last I was involved with. He's one of my favourites, along with Bob Cryer and Frank Burnside – I'm particularly proud of them.

"And although I'm no longer closely involved with the production, I really admire the way the team have developed *The Bill*. I think it's terrific stuff."

getting himself suspended on his first day when, in the old fashioned way, he clipped a youngster round the ear. Thankfully, for Carver, the lad's father agreed with the punishment and nothing further was made of the incident. The play also examined the conflict that exists between the two sides of many police stations: the uniform branch and the CID. *Old Bill* was considered perhaps a little too offensive to the police and the title was changed to *Woodentop* – the CID's nickname for any-one wearing the blue serge uniform.

Woodentop was to be directed by Peter Cregeen, a vastly experi-enced director who, in the previous twenty years, had been involved with most of the successful British TV police series – from *Z Cars* and *Softly, Softly* to *Juliet Bravo* and *The Gentle Touch*. However, when Cregeen opened Geoff McQueen's script, he initially felt an all too familiar sense of dissapointment. "I just couldn't believe there was room for yet another police-based story," he recalls. "Surely every possible permutation had been covered over the years."

But gradually, as he turned the pages, he began to realise that here was something new. "I was delighted to find that Geoff's script had a great freshness and a sense of immediacy to it. It also had a different approach which, to my mind, truly reflected present day society in the metropolitan area of London."

In 1982 a fine documentary series *The Police* – made by Roger Graef, about the Thames Valley force – had been broadcast by the BBC. Using a 'fly-on-the-wall' technique, these films took the viewer into the everyday lives of the boys in blue. Like most TV professionals

---

Complete Cast of *Woodentop*

PC Jim Carver	Mark Wingett
PC Litten	Gary Olsen
WPC Ackland	Trudie Goodwin
Sgt Wilding	Peter Dean
Insp Deeping	Jon Croft
DI Galloway	Robert Pugh
PC Morgan	Colin Blumenau
Duty Sergeant	Chris Jenkinson
Duty PC	Richard Huw
Winston Summers	Paul McKenzie
Reg Taylor	Gary Hailes
George Taylor	Colin McCormack
1st Neighbour	Dawn Perllman
2nd Neighbour	Maryann Turner
Caretaker	Derek Parkes
Executive Producer	Lloyd Shirley
Producer	Michael Champman
Director	Peter Cregeen

WPC Ackland (Trudie Goodwin) in *Woodentop* with Sergeant Wilding played by Peter Dean who later became Pete Beale in *Eastenders*.

Cregeen had been highly impressed by Graef's no-holds-barred work. The director also realised that the showing of the Thames Valley series would strongly influence the future of all police drama on television. "Its absolutely free-wheeling style of camerawork was so vivid and alive, that there was no way we could produce a police-based story like the old ones used to be."

And so, bearing *The Police* example very much in mind, *Woodentop* was made, using a hand-held camera, realistic sets and a minimum of naturalistic lighting. "It wasn't shot dramatically, as a film would be," said Peter Cregeen. "I felt that the compulsion to view should come from the dramatic situations as written, and from the way in which the police dealt with them. The camera was there simply to observe all of this as it happened."

Included in the cast were Mark Wingett, as the idealistic new recruit Jimmy Carver, Trudie Goodwin as WPC June Ackland, Colin Blumenau as PC 'Taffy' Morgan, Peter Dean as Sergeant Wilding, Gary Hailes as the young tearaway whose ear is clipped by Carver, and Robert Pugh as a 'Brummie' DI Galloway. Both Peter Dean and Gary Hailes were destined for further fame in *EastEnders*.

Woodentop was transmitted in the autumn of 1983 and met with critical acclaim. Thames were quick to realise that Geoff McQueen, Michael Chapman and Peter Cregeen had between them produced a potential contender in the everlasting ratings war. And, a month after the transmission of *Woodentop*, the company decided to expand the basic idea into a series of twelve 60-minute episodes. Reverting to a revised version of Geoff McQueen's original title, the series was to be called *The Bill*.

2 Funny Ol' Business Cops and Robbers

It was decided that *The Bill* would continue the basic format of *Woodentop*. Episodes would be multi-stranded so they could refect as accurately as possible both the routine work and diversity of cases dealt with by a single relief in a typical Metropolitan police station. It was also decided right from the start that every scene in *The Bill* would be experienced through the eyes of the police, their emotions and feelings; *everything* would be seen from a police viewpoint. For instance, viewers will never see a gang of villains planning a robbery; nor a traffic accident as it happens (unless a police officer is present), they will only see the effects that the robbery or the accident have on the police officers sent to deal with it.

Nor would *The Bill* enter the homes of the officers, unless the storyline absolutely demanded it. Should a police officer be experiencing a particular private or domestic problem, then the viewer would see the effect that problem had on that officer's ability to do his or her job.

Together, Geoff McQueen and producer/script editor Michael Chapman created several new characters to increase the staff of Sun Hill and the new roles were painstakingly cast to match with those actors retained from *Woodentop*: Mark Wingett, Trudie Goodwin, Gary Olsen and Colin Blumenau (whose character name was changed from 'Morgan' to 'Edwards'). DI Galloway, previously portrayed as a Midlander by Robert Pugh, became a Cockney to bring him closer to the reality of John Salthouse who now took over the role.

Early in 1984 McQueen began work on three episodes of the series. The remaining scripts would come from Barry Appleton, who wrote seven episodes, and John Kershaw who penned one story. The planned twelfth episode was never completed because of industrial action.

Meanwhile, construction work had begun on *The Bill*'s first production unit – housed in a single-storey warehouse and office complex in Artichoke Hill, Wapping, East London. The building stood behind Rupert Murdoch's News International plant, home of the *Sun*, the *News of the World*, *The Times* and the *Sunday Times*. The work was completed in the spring and recording of the first hour-long episodes began in late-March in the newly created Sun Hill and at locations in the vicinity of Artichoke Hill.

Many Thames staffers dreaded the thought of being sent to this

Sergeant Cryer and WPC
Ackland with DI Galloway
(John Salthouse) in an early
episode of *The Bill*.

East End outpost, but those who did work on *The Bill* soon began to
enjoy the team spirit that was apparent right from the start – and were
quick to appreciate the sense of autonomy enjoyed by the unit. The
building was somewhat cramped and certain production offices had to
'double' as parts of Sun Hill. For example, Michael Chapman's office
was also Chief Superintendent Brownlow's office, and the canteen
was used both in the programme and by cast and crew. As one Sun
Hill insider recalls, "The shoot always took priority and, no matter
who you were or where you were, if your office was needed then you
moved out."

The first episode of *The Bill*, 'Funny Ol' Business – Cops and
Robbers', was broadcast at 9pm on Tuesday 16 October 1984. The
story plunged its viewers into the workaday routines of Sun Hill police
station, situated in an unspecified borough of London's East End.
The first words of the series were spoken by Sergeant Alec Peters
(Larry Dann) as he handed over the relief to Sergeant Bob Cryer
(Eric Richard) who in turn proceeded to conduct the morning parade,
reminding his squad about the recent spate of car thefts, pickpocket-
ing and break-and-enter burglaries proliferating in the district.

As the story unfolded it was quickly apparent that *The Bill* was
something different. Right from the start it seemed 'real'. The performances were fresh, the acting had an earthy, improvised feel about it;
while the camera-work, mostly hand-held and certainly very mobile
and free-wheeling, was exciting and documentary-like.

Yet who among the production team or the cast of the first episode,

Larry Dann as Sergeant Peters spoke the first lines in *The Bill* when he handed over the relief to Sergeant Cryer, played by Eric Richard.

would have dared to predict the eventual popularity and longevity of *The Bill*? After all, as Peter Cregeen had already observed, police-based stories were nothing new.

So why did *The Bill* catch on so quickly?

Obviously, part of the answer lies in the excellence of the production, from writing through to editing; another part in the curiosity value offered by the new realistic approach of *The Bill*; another in the fact that the storylines were not reliant on the superficiality of mere plot and effect, as so many police dramas had been in the past. *The Bill* was definitely 'character driven': almost immediately the audience met characters in whom they could believe and with whom they could identify – an essential ingredient to any genuine drama.

Yet a further factor lay in the *timing* of those first transmissions. Throughout the early-1980s the British police had figured more prominently than usual in the national headlines. In January 1980 a 'Flying Squad' detective had been jailed for attempting to bribe another officer. Later that year a number of officers were injured in a riot in the St Paul's district of Bristol; and a police officer was among the hostages held captive during the siege of the Iranian embassy which had begun at the end of April.

1981 saw the eventual arrest and life imprisonment of Peter Sutcliffe, dubbed 'The Yorkshire Ripper'. The investigating police were heavily criticised for previously allowing him to slip through their net. It was also the year of the riots in Brixton and Toxteth and the shooting of PC Olds.

Roger Graef's TV series *The Police*, so influential to the style of *The Bill*, was first shown in 1982. That summer Michael Fagan evaded security networks at Buckingham Palace and found his way into the Queen's bedroom. The Sergeant on duty at the time was later transferred.

In January 1983, in Kensington, Stephen Waldorf was shot by Detectives who had mistaken him for a suspected armed robber. The incident highlighted certain weaknesses in the Metropolitan Police firearms training.

As work was starting on *The Bill* at the beginning of 1984, the Police and Criminal Evidence Act (PACE) was passed by Parliament in a cloud of controversy (the act would come into effect two years later). In April '84 WPC Yvonne Fletcher was shot dead while on duty during a demonstration outside the Libyan Embassy in St James's Square, London. In May, police and pickets clashed at Orgreave, South Yorkshire, during the miners' strike.

All of these incidents reminded the public of the fact that police work is often dangerous, sometimes controversial. And the timing was right to reflect these factors more realistically than ever before in terms of television drama.

The 'timing' factor is further underlined by the fact that 'Funny Ol' Business – Cops and Robbers' was broadcast as detectives were sifting through the rubble of the Grand Hotel in Brighton, in their search for clues into the terrorist bombing which had almost decimated the government of the country only four days earlier.

As the series progressed throughout the remainder of 1984, the storylines – covering such subjects as bomb hoax phone calls, indecent assault, firearms control, drug-dealing, jewel theft, 'domestic' problems, pornography and murder – were intertwined with insights into the internal politics of the station: the guarded suspicion between the uniformed officers and the CID personnel, the unspoken yet obvious respect shown by the young constables towards Sergeant Bob Cryer, the turning of a blind eye and the bending of the rules as occasionally observed by DI Dave Galloway (John Salthouse) and his CID-men.

By mid-January 1985, when the first series came to a close, Thames had commissioned Series Two with Peter Cregeen taking over the Producer's role from Michael Chapman, who had left to produce *Mr Palfrey of Westminster*, which also began as a *Storyboard* project.

The first episode of Series Two 'Snouts & Red Herrings', written by Geoff McQueen and directed by Peter Cregeen, was broadcast on 11 November 1985. As the series progressed it showed a marked improvement over Series One; the writing – by Geoff McQueen, Barry Appleton, Ginnie Hole, Christopher Russell, Lionel Goldstein, Tim Aspinall and Jim Hill – was tighter, the regular characters more established and well-defined. And by the time of the transmission of episode twelve – Barry Appleton's 'The Chief Superintendent's Party' – on 10 February 1986, *The Bill* was firmly established as a television success story.

A third series was commissioned and plans were laid for transmis-

Among *The Bill's* keenest fans are Jan Daniels and Dianne Strachan who between them produce *Sierra Oscar*, a regular 'letterzine'. Within a year of its launch, circulation of *Sierra Oscar* was hovering around the 2,000 mark, and rising. Incorporated within '*SO*' is a section devoted to UBAS (the Unofficial Bill Appreciation Society). Many Sun Hill insiders believe that it's high time Jan and Di's efforts were recognised officially.

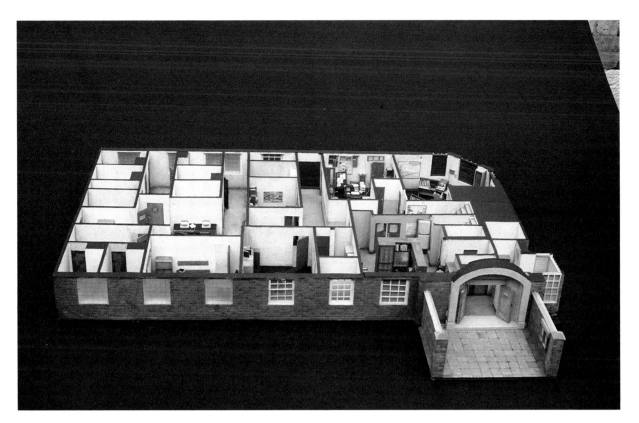

A detailed model of Sun Hill mark II (Barlby Road) which can now be seen in the Museum of the Moving Image in London.

sion in late '86, which meant that recording would have to take place early in that year. But, as the theme song to another well-known TV show persists in telling us, 'everybody needs good neighbours' – and it transpired that events concerning the people next door were about to have a knock-on effect which would eventually bring production of *The Bill* to a complete standstill.

During the break in the production schedule in the winter of '85-86, the highly publicised print workers' strike errupted at the neighbouring News International plant. When the Sun Hill production line began to roll again, picket lines and police were in confrontation virtually on the doorstep. There were even a few awkward instances of uniformed cast members actually, and understandably, being mistaken for real policemen.

Thames were obviously hoping that the dispute would be resolved quickly, so that things could return to normal. Instead, the strike escalated into a long, drawn out affair. The streets around 'Fortress Wapping' were blocked off and barbed-wire barricades sprouted up all over the area. It became an intolerable sitution for *The Bill* – and the problem was worsened by the fact that a new block of flats was under construction nearby. It was eventually decided that production of Series Three would have to be suspended until a new 'Sun Hill' could be found. (Ironically, when *The Bill* moved out of Artichoke Hill the real police moved in, using the building as a temporary base.)

By October 1986 work had begun on a new base for *The Bill* – in a former record company distribution depot in Barlby Road, North

Kensington. The shooting of Series Three finally began in March 1987. And by the time Geoff McQueen's 'The New Order of Things', the first episode of the series, was eventually transmitted in September, fans of *The Bill* had been without their favourite programme for nineteen months. Series Three ran from 21 September 1987 to 7 December 1987.

By then the decision had already been taken by Thames to upgrade *The Bill* into a twice-weekly half-hourly format, to begin transmission in the summer of '88.

Series Three had ended with a bang. The last hour-long episode – 'Not Without Cause', written by Barry Appleton – was a tense drama which ended with Sergeant Tom Penny (Roger Leach) being shot in the stomach by an old lady protecting her flat against an unscrupulous landlord.

The transition between the hour and half-hour episodes was handled quite brilliantly with the first short episode – 'Light Duties' by Geoff McQueen – broadcast on 19 July, showing the slowly recovering Tom Penny putting a brave face on things as he tries to conceal his pain. The story also saw the arrival at Sun Hill – a day early and in civilian clothes – of Inspector Christine Frazer (Barbara Thorn), and DS Ted Roach's (Tony Scannell) attempt to chat her up in Sun Hill's local pub.

Roger Leach, who played Sergeant Penny, now writes scripts for the programme.

Firearms used in *The Bill* are specially hired. Occasionally real weapons are used, although replica guns are more usual.

The first organised police force were the 'Bow Street Runners'. This small group of 'thief takers' was recruited in 1750 by Henry Fielding, the second magistrate of Bow Street court in London and noted author of *Joseph Andrews* and *Tom Jones*.

Fielding's men performed their public-spirited duty unpaid, except for the occasional reward of 'blood money' handed over on the recovery of stolen property or the successful arrest of a wrong-doer.

The 'Bow Street Runners' wore no official uniform, but were recognised by the long tipstaff of a parish constable which they invariably carried. Despite their meagre numbers, they were effective in helping to quell at least some of the crime that was rampant in eighteenth-century London. The 'Runners' measure of success, albeit modest, led to calls for a permanent and professional police force in London.

In 1812 Robert Peel, a 23-year-old Tory MP, was appointed Secretary for Ireland where he formed the Irish Constabulary, a body which became known as the 'Peelers'. By 1825 Peel had been given the task of reforming the criminal law in England. Four years later, after encountering a great deal of prejudice

from within the government, his work led to the formation of the Metropolitan Police Force in 1829, with its first official uniform of blue tailcoat and trousers and a black top hat.

During the next twenty years other forces were formed in other British cities and counties, but it took almost thirty years for the police force to become generally accepted by the public. By then they were affectionately known, at least by law abiding citizens, as 'Bobbies' in honour of Sir Robert Peel – the nickname, of course, survives today among other less affectionate.

Three favourite explanations for the derivation of the nickname 'Old Bill' as applied to policemen, are:

(1) That it comes from King William IV whose reign encompassed the founding of The Metropolitan Police.
(2) That the early police presented 'clients' with a Bill
(3) A certain East End copper who was rather partial to a glass or two of beer. His daughter would be sent to fetch him home from one of a number of local pubs, pushing open the door she would cry: "Anyone seen old Bill?"

It was a seamless transition, keeping perfect continuity with the past, accurately reflecting the personnel changes that all police stations go through from time to time – and setting the tone for the future of the series. Since then more than 350 half-hour episodes have been produced and broadcast week in and week out.

The summer of '89 saw a personnel change at the top of the production ladder when Peter Cregeen, by then elevated to the position of Executive Producer, left Thames to become Head of Series Drama at the BBC. He was succeeded as Executive Producer at Barlby Road by the *The Bill's* original producer Michael Chapman.

Also in 1989, the owners of the Barlby Road site announced that they intended to redevelop the property and turn it into a trendy covered market. Most people involved with the programme had grown very fond of the Barlby Road Sun Hill. It had about it exactly the right kind of dowdy police station atmosphere; it was reasonably

As with real policemen, the Sun Hill regulars like to take a break from the beat every now and then. But even holidays have to fit smoothly into the production cycle. "We have 27 regular characters, and that means 27 holidays," says Nigel Wilson, Project Co-ordinator. "I have to ensure that these arrangements don't put too great a strain on the system. That would certainly happen if too many of the male PCs were away at the same time – it's the same with the CID. There have to be enough 'bodies' to do the job all year round, just like any police station."

The system also allows cast members to take on other work from time to time. Eric Richard, Jon Iles and Peter Ellis, amongst others, have all appeared in theatrical productions during sabbaticals from Sun Hill.

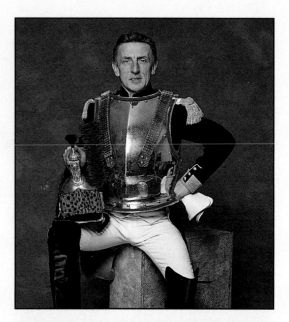

accessible for cast and crew – and it was a friendly enough place in which to work. Nevertheless, sentiment has no place in business and Thames were left with no option but to find a third Sun Hill site.

Even in a city the size of London it proved extremely difficult to find another vacant building of approximatley the same period and of more or less the same geographical configuration, and that also had enough space in which to recreate the police station and house the

Mark Powley played PC
Ken Melvin, who was killed
outside Sun Hill in a bomb
explosion.

various departments that are so essential to the production. Eventually several sites were considered and rejected. Then a firm favourite began to emerge in the Sun Hill Stakes, and for a while everyone belived they would be re-housed in a disused hospital in Clapham. But that deal fell through and Thames eventually settled on the second favourite, a former wine distribution warehouse further out in London's south-western suburbs.

The move was to be made in March 1990, and it called for an immense logistical exercise, including the creation of an extra Unit – the Green Unit – which produced 20 extra episodes during the summer of '89 to cover the eventual non-shooting weeks of the re-location. The plan also involved the *on-screen*, large-scale modernisation and refurbishment of Sun Hill. Episodes continued with overalled painters, decorators, carpenters and electricians beavering away in the background. At one point almost the entire the staff were seen to be temporarily re-housed in Portakabins in the yard as their own offices were being altered

Over the years the Sun Hill police station has generated an intricate history – and it is all recorded and stored on computer by *The Bill's* Archivist, Ruth Parkhill. She compiles a synopsis of each epsiode at the shooting script stage and her continually growing 'casebook' is often referred to by Scriptwriters, Script Editors, Casting Directors and Directors. Ruth also compiles files detailing the individual development of all the regular characters.

Apart from spreading the word regarding individual episodes, Wendy Tayler, the Unit Publicist, arranges all newspaper and magazine interviews for the cast, as well as photo sessions, personal appearances and radio and TV chat-show dates. She also distributes the sackloads of personal fan mail addressed to individual cast members, conducts studio and location press visits, deals with queries from public and police – and is involved in arranging fixtures for *The Bill's* cricket and football teams which play in many charity matches around London.

– only the CAD room remained fully operational while the recreation room doubled as a temporary canteen. Any prisoners were banged-up in the cells at the neighbouring Barton Street station.

Meanwhile, Mark Powley – who portrayed PC Ken Melvin – had decided to leave the series to pursue his career in other areas. The production team took the opportunity to use his departure to the best possible dramatic effect. Melvin met his untimely end in a bomb explosion while preparing to park a booby-trapped car in the yard. The explosion 'destroyed' parts of Sun Hill, thereby necessitating even more rebuilding work.

The entire refurbishment project was a masterful way of disguising the move to the new premises, in the most dramatic way possible. Some episodes were shot in part at the Barlby Road site and partly at the new Sun Hill, causing a kind of controlled mayhem behind the scenes. No-one at Sun Hill Mark III ever wants to repeat the moving experience.

3 Impersonating a Police Station

When creating *The Bill*, Geoff McQueen borrowed the name for his fictional police station from Sun Hill, a well-known street in his home town of Royston, Hertfordshire. Since then, as we have seen, the most famous 'nick' in Britain has actually occupied three separate sites. And reality shows that the present home of *The Bill*, a former wine warehouse in South London, has never boasted a particularly sunny aspect (its facade faces north and the walls are practically windowless), nor is it set on a hill.

But, so accurate is the work of the Design Department that, take away all the paraphernalia necessary for a television production and you'd swear you were in a real English police station with its slightly dowdy appearance and its atmosphere of impending doom.

In television production terms the complex is unique. There are no 'sets' at Sun Hill, no rooms with an invisible 'fourth wall' which is a usual feature of a TV studio. Each room in the 'station' appears precisely as it would in reality, a situation made possible by the lightweight camera, sound and lighting systems used in the production of the programme. The designers have achieved the perfect impersonation of a police station.

The cast have grown accustomed to the place, just as any real police officer comes to accept his or her 'nick' as almost a second home. And so important is the building to the success of the programme that Executive Producer Michael Chapman has often been heard to refer to Sun Hill as "the twenty-eighth character in *The Bill*".

In the series most visitors to Sun Hill enter via the FRONT PORCH, first crossing a car parking area and passing the station's flag pole and the obligatory blue lamp mounted on a lamp-post near the 'street'. A cousin to this lamp can be seen outside every police station in Britain.

Whenever the porch is not required for recording, the lamp and the 'SUN HILL' sign are removed to prevent any members of the public from innocently mistaking the building for the real thing – although this has happened several times during shooting. One old lady tried to hand in a stray dog at 'Sun Hill' and it took a long explanation to convince her to take the pup elsewhere. On another occasion a rookie postman attempted to deliver the mail for the real local police station to the receptionist at 'Sun Hill'. He turned as red as a pillar box when he realised his mistake.

The FRONT OFFICE contains a waiting area with seats, two counters – one open, for dealing with routine enquiries such as people handing in lost property; the other in a glass booth for discussing matters more private. The constable on duty – Sun Hill's initial contact with members of the public – sits behind the counters ready to deal with 'customers', one at a time. After visually appraising visitors as they come in, the constable will then approach the counter to answer the query.

All incoming information is collected and collated in the CAD (Computer Aided Despatch) ROOM where two shirt-sleeved officers, wearing telephone headsets, operate a console of VDU screens. One deals with any incoming telephone calls from the public and all personal radio calls from officers out on the beat. The other receives and sends messages to and from Scotland Yard, including instructions to deal with local '999' calls. All information and data filed through the system is eventually stored on the central police computer at Hendon.

The CAD ROOM Sergeant sits at another console on which he monitors the workload of the two operators, and is able to intervene or override any action they may take.

The COLLATOR'S OFFICE, now known officially as the LOCAL INTELLIGENCE OFFICE, or LIO, (but still called the Collator's Office by one and all) is strictly out-of-bounds to the general public – only bona fide police officers are allowed to enter this treasure trove of local knowledge. All station books and local intelligence reports are filed here. Pinned to the walls are various 'mug shots' and detailed maps of the district.

The Collator – PCs Reg Hollis, Cathy Marshall and Ron Smollett have all held the job – is familiar with the various files and any anomalies of the filing system. He or she often proves a quick source of useful information for officers conducting a case, and is also responsible for assessing and passing on any relevant information to Scotland Yard. The Collator's Office is also used for relief parades.

The INCIDENT ROOM swings into action whenever a case calls for a complex operation. For example, during a complex and long-running murder investigation, the room would become the nerve centre of the operation.

The male and female TOILETS are often seen in the series, either as places of sanctuary or for the all-important 'private word', and the whispered passing on of snippets of station gossip.

The DUTY INSPECTOR'S OFFICE is occupied by Inspector Monroe, while across the corridor Bob Cryer rules his domain from the DUTY SERGEANT'S OFFICE.

The male and female LOCKER ROOMS are practically identical, and are distinguished only by the subjects of the pin-up pictures stuck to the locker doors. Pictures of Richard Gere, Mel Gibson and Harrison Ford dominate in the female room, while the male equivalent is decorated with pin-ups of a more explicit nature.

Of course, many of Sun Hill's 'guests' would rather be somewhere else entirely – especially those who were bundled in at the back door

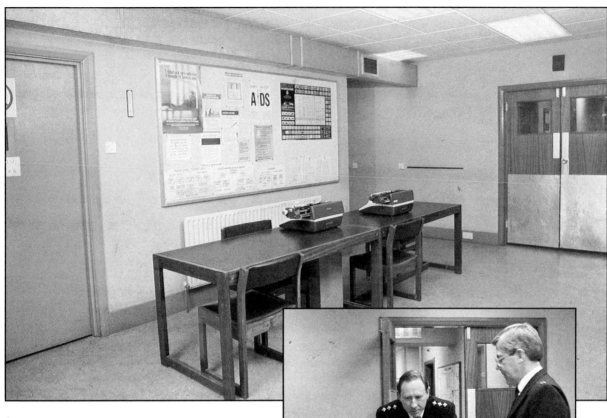

to be held for questioning. Prisoners are initially taken to the most frequently used part of the station, the CUSTODY AREA, where their personal details are noted by the Custody Sergeant. The reason for arrest is heard, followed by any explanation given by the prisoner. They are then either 'banged-up' in a cell, taken to an interview room for interrogation, or charged and cautioned on the spot. All Custody Records (previously known as Charge Sheets) are stored in the CUSTODY AREA OFICE.

The station's eight CELLS, nondescript and small, are quite bare except for a bed and a toilet. Each door has a wicket 'peephole' so that officers can keep a watchful eye on the prisoner within. Four of the cells are for male occupancy, two for females, and two, less forbidding, for the detention of juveniles.

Also in the cell area is the FINGERPRINT ROOM, complete with all the necessary inky apparatus required for the job. When necessary, prisoners' photographs are also taken in here.

Any injuries are treated in the DOCTOR'S ROOM which is equipped to First Aid standard. All police officers up to the rank of Inspector are required to hold a current First Aid Certificate and can therefore deal with any minor injuries. For anything more serious either the Divisional Surgeon (known as the Police Doctor, usually a

SUN HILL PERSONNEL
Chief Supt. Charles Brownlow
Chief Insp. (Operations) Derek Conway

UNIFORM

Insp. Andrew Monroe

Duty Sgt. Bob Cryer (92)
Sgt Alec Peters (96)
Sgt John Maitland (63)
Sgt Matthew Boyden (79)

WPC June Ackland (643)
WPC Norika Datta (181)
WPC Suzanne Ford (659)
WPC Delia French (832)
PC George Garfield (218)

PC Reg Hollis (171)
PC Stephen Loxton (363)
WPC Cathy Marshall (487)
PC Dave Quinnan (340)
PC Tony Stamp (595)
PC Barry Stringer (577)

Collator: PC Ron Smollett (330)

CID

DCI Kim Reid

DI Frank Burnside

DS Alistair Greig
DS Ted Roach

DC Jim Carver

DC Mike Dashwood
DC Alfred Lines
WDC Viv Martella

Plus various uniformed male and female personnel behind the scenes but not normally featured in the series. These include civilian Scene Of Crime Officers (S.O.C.O.); traffic wardens; Brownlow's secretary (Marion) and his clerk; Administration Sergeant; two general secretaries; three canteen/kitchen staff; two early morning cleaners and a general purpose handyman.

Relief times
UNIFORM
Early: 0600–1400
Late: 1400–2200
Night: 2200–0600

CID
1000–1800
1400–2200
(flexible)

Officers up to and including the rank of Chief Inspector can work paid overtime, if necessary

Sergeant Matthew Boyden played by Tony O'Callaghan.

The Sun Hill division is divided into twenty beats which, in turn, are further divided into five 'home beats' containing four beats each. An officer will normally maintain the same home beat for at least two years.

local GP on a retainer) is brought in, or an ambulance is called for.

Suspects and witnesses are questioned in one of Sun Hill's INTERVIEW ROOMS – impersonal and bare except for a table, chairs and a tape recorder. For security purposes the officer conducting the interview is always accompanied by a fellow officer. If the interviewee is a female, then one of the attendant officers must also be a female.

The PROPERTY OFFICE is an Aladdin's Cave of carefully logged items which have perhaps been found in the street and handed in at the front office or are there as a result of crimes and are waiting to be used in evidence. The Property Officer who logs, bags and secures all this booty is a civilian, usually a retired police officer. The items are actually supplied by *The Bill's* Property Department who will scour the city for any object called for by a script, no matter how obscure.

The all-important CANTEEN is at its busiest in three shifts, between 8.00am-10.30am, 12.00 noon-2.00pm and 5.00pm-7.00pm. Cast, crew and other production staff dine in the canteen, unless it has been requisitioned for recording purposes – in which case, catering is provided on double-decker buses in the car park. The Canteen windows are of darkened glass, so that recording can take place regardless of the lighting conditions outside.

Adjoining the canteen is the RECREATION ROOM, complete with snooker table, dart board and computer game. This location also doubles in the series and in reality – and it is said that whenever anyone wants to find Mark Wingett, they need look no further!

The CID OFFICE contains the desks of Grieg, Roach, Dashwood, Lines, Carver and Martella and is connected to the private office of DI Burnside. Their boss DCI Kim Reid has her own private office within earshot.

Ideally, three Sergeants will be on duty at Sun Hill in each relief, the most important being the CUSTODY SERGEANT who sits in the Custody Area and deals with all prisoners. His work is governed by PACE and his position gives him the authority to question the actions of ranks senior to himself. The CAD ROOM SERGEANT oversees all messages received and sent by the station, while the SECTION SERGEANT supervises all street duty officers. Sergeants will alternate these jobs among themsleves, and will usually fill a particular role for a week at a time. If for any reason a full compliment of three Sergeants is not available on a particular relief, then the Section Sergeant will invariably take on the duties of the Custody Sergeant.

The DUTY SERGEANT (Bob Cryer) monitors and controls the duties of all four station reliefs and basically ensures that there are enough 'bodies' to do the job. He also handles any licensing work – such as a pub application for extension of drinking hours.

The Sergeants are directly responsible to the DUTY INSPECTOR (Andrew Monroe) who, in turn, is ultimately responsible for all uniformed policing on Sun Hill's 'ground' during his tour of duty.

We are now treading Sun Hill's corridors of power and peeking into the plusher surroundings enjoyed by Chief Inspector Derek Conway – the man who runs Sun Hill. Next door is the largest, plushest office of all, that of Chief Superintendent Charles Brownlow, which in turn adjoins the CONFERENCE ROOM, complete with cocktail cabinet and conference table. This room is often used for formal and informal meetings and for entertaining local dignitaries or

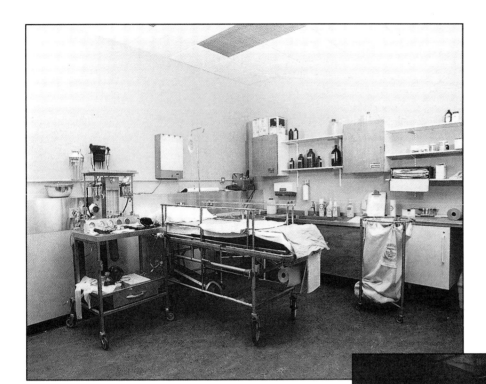

visiting high ranking officers from Area Command.

Outside in the YARD are several car parking spaces for the use of official vehicles only – although the Chief Superintendent, the Chief Inspector and the DCI can park there with impunity. Anyone else attempting to park a private vehicle in this area would be promptly ordered to shift it. Prisoners are invariably brought in via the yard, which leads directly into the Custody Area.

The Sun Hill complex also contains two purpose-built sets – ST. HUGH'S HOSPITAL CASUALTY AREA with a reception and

All police vehicles in *The Bill* are supplied and maintained by a specialist company, Action Vehicles – and, as with the uniforms, are kept under the tightest security. The latest models are loaned to the company by Vauxhall, Ford and Rover. Individual vehicles are specialy 'dressed' to represent real police transport. Occasionally special vehicles – prison vans and coaches for example, are loaned from the police. Action Vehicles' manager for *The Bill* is Simon Crook.

Sun Hill officers employ two radio systems. The most frequently used is the Personal Radio system (PR), controlled and monitored by the CAD Room. A PR is carried by all officers on street duty, either on foot or in car, and is a local radio only. The second system is Radio Telephony (RT), carried on the Area Car and certain other instant response vehicles, including the Station Van, CID vehicles, general purpose cars and the cars of the Section Sergeant and the Duty Inspector. Panda cars do not usually carry an RT set. The RT system is controlled by Information Room at Scotland Yard.

Radio Call Signs

Sun Hill	Sierra Oscar

('Sierra Oscar' denotes Divisional station Sun Hill within 'S' Division)

Area car	Sierra 1
Duty Officer	Sierra Oscar 1 (Monroe)
Station van	Sierra Oscar 2
Section Sergeant	Sierra Oscar 3
Uniform (General purpose pool)	Sierra Oscar 4
CID (General purpose pool)	Sierra Oscar 5
CID (General purpose pool)	Sierra Oscar 6
CID (General purpose pool)	Sierra Oscar 7
CID (General purpose pool)	Sierra Oscar 8
Chief Superintendent	Sierra Oscar 51 (Brownlow)
Chief Inspector (Operations)	Sierra Oscar 54 (Conway)
Detective Chief Inspector	Sierra Oscar 56 (Reid)
Panda Car	Sierra Oscar 84
Panda Car	Sierra Oscar 85
Panda Car	Sierra Oscar 86
Dog van	Area 023
TSG vehicle (Uniform)	211, 212, 213, 214

waiting area, curtained cubicles and a small ward on an upper floor level; and a wood panelled COURTROOM with a corridor and ante-rooms. These more traditional studio sets, lit by a battery of arc lights, are frequently used in the storylines and save valuable production hours that would otherwise be spent in searching for suitable hospital or courtroom locations.

Sometimes art can imitate life a little too closely. For instance, an episode due for transmission might mirror some tragic event in real life (a bombing incident, or a child abduction, perhaps). Although such a situation could arise only out of pure coincidence since *The Bill* is generally planned many months ahead of transmission, it is nevertheless a possibilty which has to be borne in mind by the Executive Producer.

On each transmission day the national news is carefully monitored. An episode which could be construed as insensitve, or likely to cause any further anguish to victims or relatives, could be withdrawn and its transmission date revised.

As a young girl in Eltham, south-east London, Trudie Goodwin was captivated by the theatre, to which her parents took her and her younger brother as often as they could.

Trudie always volunteered to be in school plays, at Blackheath High Junior and later Eltham Hill Grammar, and eventually joined the Greenwich Youth Theatre before she decided to become a drama teacher. Armed with the requisite amount of 'A' level

Trudie Goodwin

passes she attended Dartington College in Devon, to study dance and drama and then went on to Exeter University to gain an English and drama degree.

"I got my first teaching post at twenty-two, in Deptford," says Trudie. "I did it for about a year but found it almost impossible to switch off at the end of the day. I wasn't really enjoying the work as I felt I should have been if it were my true vocation. Anyway, at twenty-two you still don't know what you want out of life - never mind trying to teach others. It gradually dawned on me that I really wanted to try my hand at acting. It was 'now or never' time, so I gave up teaching and effectively put myself out of full-time employment for a long while."

While working in turn as a waitress, barmaid and cleaner, Trudie sent off an endless ream of letters to theatrical companies all over the country. "The replies, from those who bothered to answer, were all negative. Eventually a friend suggested I try the field of Theatre-in-Education and I got an audition with Theatre Centre, a company which specialised in tours of schools. I think my chief asset was being able to drive and holding a current licence, but I didn't mind, I threw myself into it one hundred per-cent: I drove the van, painted the scenery, mended the costumes and acted in the shows."

Before leaving Theatre Centre over a year later, Trudie had earned her all-important Equity card and she had directed two plays for the company. She then broadened her experience with repertory work, in Worcester, Coventry, Exeter and Leicester.

It was in Leicester that she met her future husband, actor Kit Jackson. They married and lived in a small council flat in London. "We were stony broke, and between auditions I went back to part-time waitressing and bar work, while Kit worked on building sites and washed cars."

But gradually the parts began to come their way and they were eventually able to get a mortage on a flat in Brixton. Trudie made her TV debut as a secretary in the BBC's *Softly, Softly*, but her first substantial small screen role was in Thames' *Fox*, the saga of a south-London family with criminal connections, screened in 1980. "I played the girlfriend of one of the

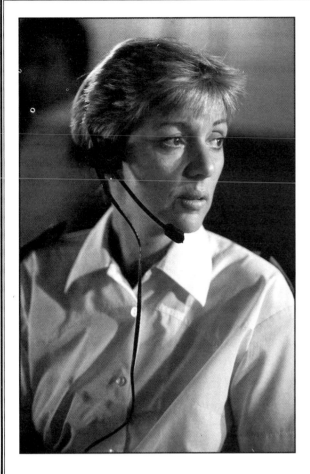

brothers and Mark Wingett was also in the cast."

Three years later Trudie and Mark teamed up once again in *Woodentop*, the play that would alter the course of both their lives. Yet, incredible though it may seem, Trudie almost didn't attend the interview which led to the job. "At the time I had only recently given birth to our first daugther, Jessica, and I was still feeling tired from getting up in the middle of the nights and all of that. Before Jessica was born I'd been doing a lot of improvised drama, and I'd appeared in *The Law Machine* for LWT and I think that combination prompted Thames to call me in for *Woodentop* - that and the fact that I wasn't a particularly well-known TV face.

"To be honest, it was a real drag going all the way across London. I didn't want to leave the baby for too long, and because I was still a little overweight

from the pregnancy I thought I'd never be offered the part of a police officer. What's more, my hair reached down to my waist. When I walked in Michael Chapman and Peter Cregeen went quiet and someone said, 'Ah...you...er...don't look anything like your Spotlight photo', and I thought, that's it. Wasted journey."

But even with all these omens seemingly stacked against her, Trudie was offered the role of WPC June Ackland - and her hair was cropped to shoulder length. "...which was still quite long for a policewoman, but since it was only a one-off play I was allowed to keep it like that."

Working on *Woodentop* turned out to be a harrowing experience for Trudie, especially in the scene in which Carver and Ackland discover the body of an old lady who had died in her bath. "At first I found it difficult to react to the 'body', so they showed Mark and I some photographs of actual bodies in various stages of decomposition. I felt sick, but had no trouble finding the right reaction after that."

Once *Woodentop* had been shot and transmitted Trudie promptly forgot all about it and was pleasantly surprised when offered a regular spot in *The Bill*. "Then the hair had to be cut really short and it's stayed that way ever since."

June Ackland went on to become one of the mainstays of the programme, and was once described - along with Sergeant Cryer - as the closest thing Sun Hill has to a perfect police officer. "Actually I think she's too involved in the job - which is why she's so good at it," says Trudie. "I think she's accepted her lot in life - she could become a Sergeant, but that would entail all the exams and stuff and I really don't think she can be bothered with all that. And when she did ask Conway what were her chances of promotion, she received an evasive reply, which really told her the answer.

Anyway, promotion would mean her moving to another station - and that would not be good for me."

Along with the stresses and strains of the job at Sun Hill, June also had the added burden of looking after her sick father. When he died in hospital she reacted by getting seriously drunk while supposedly on duty. In sympathy, Sergeants Cryer and Penny covered for her and put her in the hotel sauna to sober up.

"Poor June. Losing her father changed her social life, but it's been quite disastrous. She was able to go out more in the evenings, she was suddenly free. But her affair with DCI Gordon Wray (Clive Woods) was doomed right from the start, because he was married. Such an affair in the Force is known as going 'over the side' or 'OTS': it's an occupational hazard. This one became a prime item of station gossip and led to Wray being transferred with his chances of future promotion effectively ruined and June's reputation somewhat blackened."

June's fortunes took a further dive when she was punched and kicked while attempting to arrest a drug pusher during a disturbance on the Jasmin Allen Estate. "Incensed by the attack, perpetrated by the estate's Community Representative Everton Warwick, she then brought an ABH suit against him. And when the police authorities refused to back her she proceeded with a Public Prosecution which she ultimately lost - she therefore has very little money left in the bank. She really is an unhappy girl."

Certain *Bill* locations have stuck in Trudie's mind over the years. "We did an episode in a mortuary once, and it was foul. It's a smell you never ever forget - the smell of death. Of course, police officers eventually get accustomed, immune, to it but I don't think I ever could. Another was shot in a huge

chicken coop, in the hottest week of the year. The temperature outside was in the high 80s; inside it was even hotter and by the end of the week it really reeked in there."

If Trudie Goodwin was originally chosen for *Woodentop* because she 'wasn't a particularly familiar TV face', that's certainly no longer the case. Her brilliant portrayal of sad June Ackland means that she's now recognised far and wide. "Once on a location in London, a lady came up to me and asked if I'd put in a good word for her son who had been arrested for something or other and had been taken to the local nick.

"We went on holiday to Italy a few years ago - and I was spotted straight away by some railway workers in Milan. And in the summer of 1991 I was windsurfing on a lake in the middle of France when another windsurfer passed by in the opposite direction. He saw me and yelled 'Aren't you the woman in *The Bill*?' I was so taken aback that I fell off my board."

How does Trudie manage to maintain the consistency and spontenaiety of her performance? "Even if you're merely standing in the background with nothing to say, you have to think out your reactions to whatever is happening in the scene. It's no good thinking about what you've got to get from Sainsbury's or what you've got to do at home. Do that, and the performance would not ring true. The only way I can survive as June Ackland is by giving her one hundred per cent. Every time."

Before landing the role of Charles Brownlow in *The Bill* Peter Ellis had his own preconceived notions about the rank of Chief Superintendent, as have most people who have had no close involvement with the police. "I suppose I thought of Chief Supers as a breed of slightly-out-of-touch figureheads," said Peter. "And what's more, the original character description of Brownlow described him as 'a limited, conventional, unimaginitive man'. (Not a lot to act there, I thought.)"

It therefore came as a pleasant shock for Peter when, during the course of his research for the role, the Chief Supers he met turned out to be quite a radical bunch. "They were not in any sense out of touch and I discovered that, if anything, the Chief Supers are the ones constantly pushing for changes in the force.

"I think there's a feeling among the lower ranks that senior officers are idiots. It's the same in the services. But they tend to forget that a Chief Superintendent has done their job, and a lot more besides, to get where he is. And in all probability he actually misses being out on the streets. If there's a big operation going on, you can bet he'd rather be out there than talking about it on the end of a phone."

And that is the essence of Charles Brownlow. Peter Ellis manages to convey a sense of brooding frustration behind Brownlow's seemingly efficient

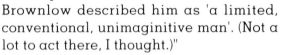

Peter Ellis

command of Sun Hill.

Yet, so well established is Peter's portrayal of the Guv'nor, that it comes as quite a surprise to learn that he originally auditioned for one of the CID roles. "I was obviously wrong for the part, a little too old, perhaps. But, as I was walking out the door, they called me back - and I was suddenly promoted to Chief Superintendent, albeit for one episode. I think the original thinking behind *The Bill* was that it would be about the guys on the beat, therefore the Senior officers wouldn't come into it very often."

But, of course, *The Bill* evolved into a drama about the entire equation of a typical London police station and it became essential for Peter's role to expand. "At first it felt like just another job, but by the end of the first series we knew it was something quite special. And now it's like working in a well-run repertory theatre with a marvellous ensemble cast."

He also enjoys the free-wheeling method of recording the programme, and was most surprised to learn that he holds the record for working on the most episodes in one week: five. "In truth, it's actually very exciting to work on one, two, even three stories at a time. It keeps the adrenalin going. And although we actors love to whinge and imagine we're never going to get through the workload, we always do."

Peter was born in Bristol in 1936, but his family moved, in turn, to London, Aldershot and Devon. He left school at fifteen and worked in various jobs including a spell in the Merchant Navy on board North Sea colliers. He became an engineeering apprentice at an aircraft factory in Farnborough, this led to an RAF flying scholarship and a place at Ruskin College, Oxford, where he read politics, philosophy and economics. And it was in Oxford that he first became interested in the theatre. "I started as an Assistant Stage Manager at the Oxford Playhouse and did my first acting in 1954 with the Elizabethan Theatre Company, which was run by Peter Hall."

A brief interlude as a civilian flying instructor was followed by three years at the Central stage school in London. Then began a long and successful career as a professional actor. He spent three years with The Old Vic Company playing, among other roles, Benvolio in Franco Zeffirelli's stage version of *Romeo and Juliet* and Hotspur in *Henry IV*. He also directed *The White Devil* at the Old Vic. During this period he was involved in an

ultimately unsuccessful attempt to ressurect the Young Vic company (others would later succeed in the venture).

Peter's first TV role was as a footman in an adaptation of John Galsworthy's *Loyalties*. He went on to make many more appearances on the small screen, including six *Wednesday Plays*, *Coronation Street*, the part of "an elderly teenage rebel" in *Dixon of Dock Green* and "a psyhcopath" in *Z Cars*. More recently he is proud to have been among the cast of Victoria Wood's classic 'soap' spoof *Acorn Antiques*. Among Peter's big screen work were parts in *A Sporting Life*, *Agatha* and *An American Werewolf in London*.

Peter's community work eventually took him to Derbyshire where he ran the Stainsby Arts Centre, from a school building in the grounds of Hardwick Hall (one fledgling actor who came to the Centre was Colin Tarrant, now *The Bill*'s Inspector Monroe).

"Then came lots of repertory work, including two years at The Leeds Playhouse, two seasons at The Nottingham Playhouse, a couple in Birmingham and then five years at the Crucible in Sheffield where I acted alongside Eric Richard."

Peter went back to the Old Vic for the world tour of Hamlet, an itinerary which included China and Australia. And in 1982 he joined the Royal Shakespeare Company, acting at Stratford and in the Barbican Theatre, London, where he once again teamed up with Colin Tarrant. "While with the RSC, I was in Peter Flannery's *Our Friends in the North* in which I played a Chief Superintendent..."

Peter - divorced in the late '70s - shares a house with two of his three sons and spends his spare time either walking, gliding or "sailing an old boat in Suffolk".

Christopher Ellison was born in Fulham, south-west London, on 16 December 1946. As a teenager he joined the Merchant Navy. "I thought I'd see the world, but ended up tending cattle on board a cargo ship," he recalls.

He later travelled to Canada and worked for a while on a ranch near Calgary then sold encyclopaedias. Back in England he worked on a demolition site, although his real ambitions at that time revolved around the art world. "I was forever drawing and wanted to become an artist, or more precisely a sculptor. I went to art college in Camberwell - and that's when I became interested in acting," he says.

Chris found a job as an Assistant Stage Manager at the Richmond Theatre and was eventually given his first part there, as Brian, the teenage son, in *Woman in a Dressing Gown*, written by Ted Willis (the creator of *Dixon of Dock Green*). That performance brought Chris to the attention of an agent and his career got properly under way.

He went on to work in repertory theatres up and down the country and became a member of the Royal Shakespeare Company. He also appeared in films and on TV, cornering a section of the market with a nice line in villainy. "My first gangster-type role was in an episode of *The Sweeney* - and I seemed to be in demand for a lot of

Christopher Ellison

similar roles after that. Even when I played a policeman, it tended to be a 'bent' one. I was making a good living at specializing in villains, although I never set out to do that."

So convincing a villain was he in *The Sweeney* that, shortly after one episode had been transmitted, his car was stopped by detectives who believed him to be an armed bank robber. "It was a case of mistaken identity," recalls Chris. "They'd obviously seen me in *The Sweeney* and got my face mixed up with that of the real villain. They couldn't belive it when I told them who I was."

Among Chris's other credits in those pre-*Bill* days were parts in *The Professionals*, *Minder*, *Widows*, *Dempsey and Makepeace*, *The Gentle Touch* and the BBC's production of *Macbeth*. He has also appeared in the films *A.D. (Anno Domini)*, *The Last Days of Pompeii*, *Give My Regards to Broad Street* and, most recently, *Buster*, with Phil Collins and Julie Walters. "During the *Buster* shoot I met Bruce Reynolds, one of the real 'Great Train Robbers', on location at the film company's version of Leatherslade Farm - the place where the gang hid out back in 1963. He told me he wished they'd come to the 'film farm' all those years ago. It was more remote than their real hideout."

Frank Burnside - alias Christopher Ellison - appeared in three episodes of the first series of *The Bill*, as a Detective Sergeant. "He was a thoroughly unpleasant piece of work," says Chris. "He was extremely unpopular in the station, everyone thought he was bent, or on the take and they were relieved when he moved on to another manor."

But not for long.

Chris was invited to take on the role on a regular basis when John Salthouse (DI Galloway) left *The Bill*. "They had to find another DI and I'm glad to say Burnside was promoted and brought back to Sun Hill. And in storyline terms I think it was a master-stroke to re-introduce someone who everyone hated."

His arrival caused ripples of annoyance throughout Sun Hill. Ted Roach - who had been temporarily promoted to Acting DI, following the departure of DI Galloway - was understandably resentful at Burnside's return as his new boss, while Bob Cryer refused to trust him any further than he could throw him. The later introductions of the keen and conscientious DS, Alistair Grieg, and WDC Viv Martella would give even more scope for conflicting relationships within the CID set-up.

But Frank Burnside definitely ruled the CID roost at Sun Hill, stamping his authority on the office and leaving no one in any doubt that he was in charge. But then the producers pulled yet another clever device out of the hat, by appointing a DCI to the station.

"Since they've brought in the DCIs - first Gordon Wray, played by Clive Wood, and then Kim Reid played by Carolyn Pickles - old Frank has had to become a lot cleverer," says Christopher. "He'd never really had anyone to control him before, and that's an obstacle he has to get around now. He does it by making Kim Reid think he's toeing the line. He's grown more devious through necessity. But, although he's being a bit more subtle inside the station, when he's off the leash and out and about he's every bit as evil as he always was - and he still gets results."

Frank Burnside also does a nice line in sharp cockney wit. Here's an exchange between WPC Suzanne Ford (Vikki Gee-Dare) and the lovable Mr Burnside as they confront a particularly vociferous woman in '*Cry Havoc*':

BURNSIDE: Stick her on.
FORD: What's the charge?
BURNSIDE: Possession of an offensive mouth.

"It's quite a challenge for the scriptwriters to come up with new Burnside-isms," says Chris. "One of my favourites was 'By the time I get a whisper into the Scrubs, he'll admit to eating Shergar'. Another was 'Who's he gonna think grassed him up...Captain Kirk?' Sometimes I get the chance to contribute a Burnside-ism or two. After playing him for so long they seem to come quite naturally to me."

Christopher Ellison did not appear in one of his favourite episodes - but another Ellison did, his son Louis. '*Grace of God*', written by P Fletcher and R Le Parmentier and directed by David Hayman, concerned a young boy - played by Louis Ellison - who was abducted by a squatter and finally rescued by Bob Cryer. "It was a great experience for Louis, his first appearance on TV," says the proud father. "The episode was shot in November '89 and he's grown considerably since then."

Also since then Chris and his wife Anita, a former singer and actress, have celebrated the arrival of Louis' little sister, Francesca. "We couldn't come up with a name for ages and then we decided to name her after Frank Burnside, she'll probably be called Frankie as she gets older. She's got lovely corkscrew blonde hair now - just like Shirley Temple."

The Ellisons live in Hove and Chris spends his weekends shopping in The Lanes in neighbouring Brighton, swimming, or sailing with friends. "I'm a real weekend sailor, I love mucking about in boats and used to own a fourteen-foot fibre-glass dinghy which I kept down on the beach. But I eventually sold it when a spot of back trouble meant I was experiencing great pain when hauling it over the shingle."

A more relaxed pastime for Chris is painting, mainly watercolours. He still retains his love of art and in 1989 provided the illustrations for two children's books written by his good friend, actor Tom Cotcher. "I also do caricatures of people on *The Bill* - in fact, Burnside's blotter on his desk at Sun Hill is covered in sketches - but they are definitely not for publication."

Whether he's in Brighton, Hove or London, Christopher Ellison is constantly recognised by fans of *The Bill*. And because he is so convincing in the role of hard-man Burnside he occasionally finds himself in awkward situations. "I always know when someone wants to pick a fight with Burnside - they usually start by saying I look a lot shorter than I do on TV and I usually make a joke of it - or give them the Burnside glare. At heart I'm not an aggressive person - and fortunately nothing really serious has ever happened in any of these confrontations."

'Right, Carver, let's do it,'

The first line spoken in Geoff McQueen's *Woodentop* at the beginning of *The Bill* saga, was delivered by Mark Wingett, to himself, as Jim Carver dragged himself out of bed for his first morning at Sun Hill.

"In those days he was an idealistic young copper, fresh out of training college," says Mark. "He was a liberal-minded lad torn between becoming a social worker or a policeman and consequently carrying a liberal attitude into policing. He believed, naively, that he could change the Force."

It proved to be an eventful first day for 'Woodentop' Carver as he was 'puppy walked' around the Sun Hill ground by WPC Ackland (Trudie Goodwin) and PC Litten (Gary Olsen). With Ackland he discovered the body of an old lady decomposing in a bath. And with Litten he chased and caught a couple of unruly

Mark Wingett

youths, but put his future in the Force in jeopardy by clipping one around the ear. Only the intervention of the wise Sergeant Wilding (Peter Dean) and the understanding attitude of the youth's father saved Carver from a formal investigation.

After that narrow escape, Jim Carver's size nine boots proceeded to walk many miles on the Sun Hill beat. He was a quick learner. He was tolerant and patient, yet had a streak of toughness about him.

To the likes of Bob Cryer and Tom Penny, Carver looked a good prospect for promotion, a likely Sergeant of the future. But in Series Three his career took a different turn, when he transferred to the CID office. "Initially it was PC Litten who had the ambition to become a detective, but when Gary Olsen left the programme, Carver became the most likely lad for a transfer. I was very pleased when that happened," says Mark. "I always found acting in a uniform to be very restricting. You imagine it takes you over the minute you put it on and it's extremely uncomfortable."

Carver has developed into a fine detective and although the experiences he's had en route may have blunted some of the edges of his inate liberalism, he still retains his integrity. "He has become more realistic than idealistic," says Mark, "which is something that must happen to all keen young coppers as time goes by. But his principles are intact.

"When Burnside wanted him to lie in court, he flatly refused. He stuck by his

guns and would not give in. His principles stuck and he was at heart the same honest Carver that he was in *Woodentop*."

There is also a hint of romance in the air for young Jim. For a long time, he and Norika Datta have shown a certain affection for one another. When Phil Young attacked her he became even more protective and threatened to kill Young. "Whether the romance develops is very much in the hands of the scriptwriters," says Mark. "But Jim and Norika have definite feelings for one another, although in the past she has always turned him away. Who knows? Perhaps she'll warm to him in the future!"

Off screen, Mark is happily settled with his girlfriend, Sharon. They live in east London, together with Sharon's son Benny and plan to marry soon.

Most of Mark's spare time is taken up with scuba diving in which he is a qualified instructor. "It all began around the time I started on *The Bill*. I went along to a club with four of my mates, but I'm the only one who went the distance on the course. I'm now the Diving Officer of my club, London Wide Divers. It's a great sport which has taken me all over the world - I was actually offered a job out in Thailand. I now find myself looking through holiday brochures for likely looking places to dive - Sharon doesn't mind as long as there's a decent beach nearby."

Mark Wingett was born in Melton Mowbray, Leicestershire, on New Year's Day 1961. His father was a naval officer whose postings took the Wingett family to Malta and Singapore as well as the less exotic Portsmouth. Mark and his brother and sister were educated in nearby Horndean. His brother, Matthew, is a TV scriptwriter who recently had his first *Bill* script accepted. "For obvious reasons Matthew didn't want it known that he was my brother when he submitted his storyline, ironically titled '*Thicker Than Water*'," says Mark. "So he sent it under the appropriate pen-name 'Matthew Brothers', although it will be transmitted with his real name on the credits."

Mark always wanted to be an actor but was put off the idea by his school's careers officer. "She got me to fill in a multiple-choice questionnaire and from my answers worked out that the best thing I could be was a zoo keeper."

But the zoological world was deprived of his talents when, as teenager Mark joined the National Youth Theatre, that - now sadly defunct - breeding ground for so much of Britain's finest young acting talent. "I was very lucky at the NYT. In the first year I was in a crowd scene, in the second year I had the lead in Peter Terson's *England, My Own*, which was seen by the casting director of the film *Quadrophenia*, The Who's rock-opera. I was seventeen at the time and was given the part of one of the Mods. It had an 'X' certificate when it was released - and I was too young to go and see it."

After *Quadrophenia* Mark found himself in demand for a number of roles including parts in *Fords on Water*, *Private Schultz*, *Take Three Women*, *Fox* (Trudie Goodwin was also in the cast) and the film *Breaking Glass*. He was twenty-two when he was seen by a Thames casting director in Tony Marchant's stage play *Welcome Home*. His performance led to an invitation to audition for *Woodentop*.

As Chief Insp. (Ops), Derek Conway is at the administrative hub of Sun Hill, he is responsible for all operational policing matters - from day-to-day routines to any special or unexpected events, such as demonstrations, raids, seige situations and so on.

"I wouldn't have old Derek's job for the world," says Ben Roberts. "I've met several real Chief Inspectors since I've been with *The Bill*, and I reckon they do one of the toughest jobs in the force."

Ben Roberts

Indeed, Ben had never considered himself to be policeman material. At the age of seventeen he left his home town, Bangor in North Wales, and went to London to study catering. "But I soon got fed up with that and decided to train as an engineer, as I'd always been mechanically minded. Later, when I was living in Bayswater, my landlord ran an ILEA drama class and I got roped in, well and truly. I enjoyed it so much that I decided to give up on the engineering and go to drama school - The Webber-Douglas Academy in Kensington."

That was in 1975 and Ben was a mature student of twenty-five. "I couldn't take it seriously at first. It felt strange being older than most of the other students, but I soon pulled myself together when the academy threatened to sling me out."

On leaving Webber-Douglas in 1978, he found a job as acting ASM at the renowned Pitlochry Festival in Scotland. "We put on seven plays, a different one every night," he recalls. "But I didn't get to do much acting ...it was mainly humping scenery about and very hard work."

One consequence of the Festival was that Ben met his future wife there. "Helen was a leading lady, and it was a case of love on first night," he says. They married in 1981 and now live with their son, Joe, in Nottingham - where Helen works as a producer for Central Television.

Ben's theatrical career grew slowly. "I ran the gamut of Theatre-in-Education, played a lot of small parts in rep all over the country and eventually settled into some serious work in the triangle of Derby, Nottingham and Leicester Playhouses. That lasted for about six years and then I began to get work in London and on TV. And when Central opened in Nottingham there was suddenly a lot of work for actors in the area."

Among other television roles, Ben appeared in *Angels*, *Hard Cases* and *Tales of Sherwood* before he was asked, in 1988, to take on the tough role of Chief Inspector Conway in *The Bill*, at the changeover to the half-hour format.

"I imagined it would be a nerve-racking thing to join a successful programme like this, to join an established cast who I'd admired for three years," he says. "And Conway was supposed to lord it over most of them right from the start. But they were all extremely nice, and helped me to settle in. And I've had a great time ever since, especially whenever I've had to deliver a good rollicking."

Now Chief Inspector Derek Conway is an integral part of the Sun Hill set up. The place just wouldn't seem the same without his almost permanent scowl. "At heart, he's a good, steady copper who aligns himself with the good old days," said Ben. "He really comes into his own in storylines which bring out his organisational talents and he is a skilled negotiator in tense situations."

But even Conway gets it wrong at times, and Ben admits he enjoys it when the stolid Chief Inspector goes over-the-top. "He made a complete prat of himself in Christopher Russell's 'Beer and Bicycles', which was directed by Nick Laughland who's done a lot of comedy in the past. Conway was determined to clean up the station's image and tighten up its efficiency, and went poking around under loose floorboards and prodding about in the hollow ceilings looking for illegal alcohol. The lads on the shift got wind of this and laid false trails for him - to prevent him from discovering their real stash of booze.

"At one point he was even caught searching through Christine Frazer's filing cabinet and pulling out an item of

her underwear. I must admit we pushed it a bit too far, and the management here hated it. But I loved the episode.

"Yes, Conway can be a strange man at times - very serious, very earnest. But then he is in a strange situation within the Sun Hill hierarchy - go above Chief Inspector and you're into some serious promotion. So, he's constantly trying to place himself in a favourable atmosphere with his superiors. This often means being quite ruthless with those below him to make sure they don't leapfrog ahead of him."

However, in 'Bones of Contention' by Susan B. Shattock, Conway was turned down for promotion, following an unfavourable appraisal from Chief Superintendent Brownlow.

"When that happened, he felt totally betrayed by Brownlow and went all hurt and miffed," said Ben. "He's now absolutely certain that he'll never get promotion and I'm hoping this will bring about a subtle change in his attitude in future. Perhaps, he'll become a bit more rebellious towards Brownlow."

Off-screen Ben relaxes by flying radio-controlled airplanes at a club in Nottingham on Sunday afternoons. Or by exercising his mechanical mind - for the past few years has been occupied with the renovation of a splendid 1963 Singer Vogue.

He and Helen hope to move soon. They have been negotiating to buy a house with a large workshop attached. "It's always been a dream of mine to have a proper engineering workshop," says Ben. "And I intend using it to renovate some old Norton motorcycles. Perhaps I'll lend one of them to Derek Conway if ever he feels the need to escape the pressures of Sun Hill."

Eric Richard was born in Margate, Kent, in June 1940, but he was brought up in Brixton and considers himself a true dyed-in-the-wool south Londoner. "I've lived there practically all my life and although I travel a great deal these days, I'm always glad to come home to Streatham," he says.

As a lad, the eldest of three brothers, Eric hated school with a passion. "I had a dreadful time: it seemed to me that teachers were there

Eric Richard

for one reason only - to beat the proverbial seven shades out of me. That's my abiding memory of all teachers except one, an English teacher who stayed at our school for just two or three months. Instead of letting us just sit there reading or writing or staring into space, she either read stories aloud to us, or got us up to enact them. I can vividly recall speaking Shylock's lines from *The Merchant of Venice*. I may remember it because it was such a different school experience, or perhaps embryonically Eric Richard the actor was lurking in there thinking 'Wow! This is the game'."

In fact, 'Eric Richard the actor' would not emerge to play the game until he was 28 years old, married with two children and managing a successful motor-accessories import/export business in south London. "That was in the late-sixties, the days of 'go fast' Minis, air horns, leather steering-wheel covers and all that. My big hobby at that time was

motor-cycling (it still is), but I felt the need to do something else as well."

The firm's book-keeper was involved in amateur theatre. "We would discuss the stage at length and eventually I decided to give it a try and joined the South London Theatre Centre in Norwood. After two or three months I realised that acting was all I really wanted to do. Although my first role rather left me with a lot to live up to - I played God, or rather the voice of God."

After such an exulted start it would seem that divine intervention might help Eric's career along. But, as with the motor trade, the parts were a long time coming. To begin with it took Eric a year to work out a strategy for making such a massive change not only to his own life, but also to those of his entire family. He realised he was unable to afford to go to drama school and would have to pay his way, while learning from experience. He began to hustle for work, knocked on doors, wrote the obligatory reams of letters to theatre companies and agencies, joined fringe groups – anything to elbow his way into his newly chosen profession.

"It wasn't until 1972 that I got my first really good parts, at the Liverpool Everyman. Alan Dosser was running the company, Jonathan Pryce was there and I shared a poky, cellar-like dressing room beneath the stage, with Tony Sher. From then on it has been a gentle progression, mainly in rep where I did a wonderful variety of 'play as cast' roles, including a time at the Crucible Theatre in Sheffield where Peter Ellis was also in the company. There was just one really bad patch around '75, when I didn't work for about nine months. That came as quite a shock after three years of regular, almost constant employment."

Despite having an expressive and obviously photogenic face, television work was also a long time coming for Eric. "I did a few commercials and little bits and pieces, but my first real camera work came in 1978 when I was given a substantial role in an episode of *The Onedin Line* - I played a villainous little character who ran off with the ship's money." Eric later appeared in *Angels*, *Mitch*, *Shoestring* and the police series *Juliet Bravo*.

Sailing on *The Onedin Line* had set Eric up nicely for his next seafaring role, in *Sho-gun* which starred Richard Chamberlain. "That was a fabulous trip, the series was based in Tokyo, and was my first experience of big-money film making - they spent something like $30 million on it. My character was one of the shipwrecked crew captured by the samurai. He got gangrene and rotted away in the bottom of a pit - so I only worked on the show for about a month.

Then came what Eric describes as "a singular piece of work", as Stan in Mike Leigh's *Home Sweet Home*. "I loved working on that, I love Mike's way of involving the actors and devising his plot through improvisation - and that role certainly gave me a higher profile in the business."

He gave another fine performance as Harry Parker in *Made in Britain*, with Tim Roth, and directed by Alan Clarke, in 1982. The following year saw Eric on tour with a small-scale touring company which also included John Salthouse. "At that time John and I shared the same agent. We were in Martin Allen's *Red*

Saturday, which was a drama about soccer. We brought it to Hampstead where it went so well that it transferred to the Royal Court's Theatre Upstairs. And during that run *The Bill*'s Casting Director came to see the play. Consequently both John and I were offered roles in the first series. Him as DI Galloway, me as Sergeant Cryer."

Right from the start, Eric enjoyed working on *The Bill*. He enjoyed the improvisational approach which, it could be argued, is not far removed from that of Mike Leigh. And by the end of the first series he was pleased with Bob Cryer's development.

"Cryer is an old-fashioned copper who's seen all the changes and successfully adapted to them," says Eric. "He may regard PACE as a case of 'throwing the

baby out with the bath-water', but he nevertheless abides by the new rules."

In 1991 Bob Cryer was appointed Duty Sergeant, not necessarily a move up the promotion ladder, but a better job in terms of it's 'gentlemanly hours' as opposed to the relief shift system.

"The new job also spells a shift in his power base," says Eric. "He's lost that 'hands-on' power on the streets. But he's gained another kind of power, akin to that of an adjutant in the Army, in that he now has the ear of the higher officers while still having access to the troops."

And these days Sergeant Cryer is rarely seen in uniform, preferring to perform his duties in plain clothes. "There was an option, but it was a decision arrived at by the Costume Department and myself. We felt that the difference between Sergeant and Duty Sergeant is such a subtle one, that the audience might not pick it up if he remained in uniform, even worse they might even have been confused by it."

Off-duty, Eric - now divorced and remarried - ensures that he puts in the obligatory five hours of flying per year required keep the Private Pilot Licence which he earned a few years ago.

And he still indulges his passion for motorcycles and is the proud owner of no less than four Italian Moto Guzzi bikes and a giant Honda Goldwing which he calls "the Cadillac of the two-wheeled world".

In 1990 this interest took Eric, and his second wife Tina, to Florida for the Daytona 200 race. While there he spent a day with the Miami Police Department. For the benefit of the photographer covering the visit for an English magazine, he walked those mean streets wearing Bob Cryer's uniform. "The uniform went down really well and I got calls of 'Cool suit, Dude' from passers-by."

Eric was accompanied by a real MPD Sergeant who showed him the real thing, not the fantasy world of Miami Vice. "Miami is arguably the most violent city in America. The cops there carry guns as a matter of course, they say they'd feel naked without one. I went along as they followed up a suspected homicide report; I spoke to a prostitute whose friend had been murdered by one of her punters; and I watched the arrests of a couple of suspected 'crack' dealers."

All in all it was an enlightening if depressing experience for Eric. "It certainly underlined the fact that I could never be a real policeman. Acting is one thing, policing another."

'Dashing', 'suave', 'sophist-icated', 'sexy' - all these superlatives, and more besides, have been used to describe Jon Iles. But when he performed his very first 'take' as DC Dashwood in the first series of *The Bill*, he tripped over a lighting cable and crashed into a filing cabinet. "I was very, very nervous and have always been a bit accident-prone," says the easy-going Iles. "And that incident is truer to my character than any of those overblown adjectives."

Jon was born into an RAF family in May 1954. "I actually entered the world in Ripon, Yorkshire, but because of my father's work we moved around a lot and I spent most of my childhood in the West Country."

He first realised his talent for acting at a school in Devon, where he also excelled at various sports and eventually became head boy. "I was one of those hideous, gauche extroverts who always made people laugh. And when I was about sixteen I was hit by the blinding revelation that you can actually act for a living."

After working hard to achieve the necessary 'A' and 'O' level passes, he enrolled at The Rose Bruford College of

Jon Iles

Speech and Drama, in Sidcup, Kent. There, in the company of other equally promising young thespians, his extrovert tendancies waned. "I definitely became a lot more reserved at drama college, but it was nose-to-the-grindstone time and I learned a great deal there."

On leaving Bruford's in 1975 Jon joined The Educational Dance/Drama Theatre of Great Britain, a theatre-in-eduction company which performed in schools all over the country. "That was a stunning learning experience and within a year, having moved on to another TIE company, I qualified for full Equity status. I was so lucky. It's so difficult to do that these days because of the dearth of work."

But then came a bleak period when - for eighteen months in 1976 and 1977 - Jon found very little work. "That was quite appalling and I came close to having a nervous breakdown. But things eventually began to improve, as they usually do. The work started to trickle in and I kept the wolf from the door by appearing in around fifty commercials over the next few years."

At that time Jon lived in St. Margaret's near Twickenham. "I had a grotty flat and no friends. The saving grace was the Turk's Head pub. But even that depressed me, especially at weekend when a constant trickle of actor 'celebs' like Dennis Waterman, Robert Powell and Robin Askwith would come in. Their presence reminded me that I was scraping a living from the repeats of my commercial for the Dutch Federation of Flower Growers, while they were starring in Zeffirelli's *Confessions of Christ's Minder* or something. Since then I've settled in Greenwich, another area which attracts actors."

Occasionally Jon was also able to indulge his taste for comedy. "I had small parts in sit-coms - *Never The Twain*, *To The Manor Born* and *Fresh Fields* and I appeared several times in *The Dick Emery Show*. I loved doing comedy, but never really had the opportunity to sink my teeth into a really funny role. And then I was sent for a casting on *The Bill*, they were looking for a smoothy-type detective for just a couple of episodes."

Gradually, the part of DC Dashwood grew and, despite that early accident with the filing cabinet, Jon has remained at Sun Hill ever since, developing Dashwood into one of *The Bill*'s most popular characters. "He's had to absorb a lot of pressure, has our Mike. He was investigated for allegedly taking money

off a snout - he was grilled for hours before the case against him was finally withdrawn. He was once held at gunpoint by an escaped con. And he often screws up on a case.

"That's all exciting stuff to play, of course, but I'd really love to explore his lighter side. After all, he has a relatively safe life with the CID - a certain amount of excitement, but not too much. Off-duty he enjoys a high-profile lifestyle - a buzzing social life, which he lives to the full. He goes off for weekends, he plays lots of sport. He has private money, a fact which the storylines have touched on from time to time. I believe he invested some of it when he was younger. And, being single, he can afford a nice flat and fashionable clothes...I just wish he could be a little happier sometimes."

Among Mike Dashwood's most memorable episodes was the splendid *'When Did You Last See Your Father'*, written by Barry Appleton, directed by Bob Gabriel, and featuring the smooth 'tec inside a living-room with a live 180lb panther. "The filming of the sequence was quite straightforward. There was actually a thick perspex screen between me and Ebony the panther, and the whole room was enmeshed in a zoo-type cage. So, I was in no danger whatsoever," recalls Jon.

However, when it came to shooting some publicity stills for the episode, it was necessary for Jon to be with Ebony - to make the pictures convincing. A special living room set was built inside a cage in the Sun Hill loading bay. A leopard was also on hand in another cage to provide companionship for Ebony. And the big cat was pacified with raw meat fed to her on the end of a bamboo pole.

"The trainer, Jim Clubb, assured me that I'd be perfectly safe providing I didn't move or try to touch the cat. After thirty-minutes of allowing her to become accustomed to my presence outside the cage, he was happy that she actually 'liked' me - and I went in and stood behind the sofa, on which she was reclining. She panicked a bit at first, got off the sofa and strolled behind it, brushing up against my legs. Then she got curious about the picture on the wall and suddenly swiped at it with a great paw. I did not move a muscle. Eventually she got back on the sofa while I sat on the arm sipping a cup of tea. Lots of pictures were taken, and then Ebony got curious about the contents of the cup and actually put her mouth around the cup, the saucer and my white-knuckled hand. It was then that Jim decided to call a halt to the proceedings..."

It was all in the line of duty for 'Dashing' Jon Iles.

WPC Norika Datta comes from a Kenyan Asian family who settled in West London in the 1950s. Her parents run a newsagents shop in Uxbridge. She has one sister who is at university reading biochemistry.

On leaving school with a few 'O' levels under her belt, Norika went to work as a junior in a local hairdressers. She worked hard but always had a nagging doubt that she was in the wrong job. By the age of twenty-one, she had had enough of pampering the salon's wealthy clientele. She knew it was time to move on to something more worthwhile, and she applied to become a WPC in the Metropolitan Police force.

Meanwhile, London-born actress Seeta Indrani had been adding a formidable list of credits to her curriculum vitae. "I started out as a dancer," she says, "training at the London School of Contemporary Dance, near Euston. I later played Cassandra, a siamese cat, in the original cast of Andrew Lloyd-Webber's *Cats* which among others also included Wayne Sleep, Paul Nicholas, Brian Blessed, Elaine Page, Sarah Brightman and Bonnie Langford."

Seeta then turned to opera, one of her great loves, and appeared at Glyndebourne in Peter Hall's production of *Orpheo Ed Euridice*. In 1982 she joined the Royal Shakespeare Company at The

Seeta Indrani

Barbican Theatre where she played the Chinese girl in *Poppy*, and Tiger Lily in the company's celebrated adaptation of *Peter Pan*, the cast also included *The Bill*'s Colin Tarrant and Peter Ellis.

Other theatrical work for Seeta included the lead in Lorca's *Belisa* at the Grove Theatre, a spell with the National Theatre, and a season and national tour with the Oxford Playhouse Company in which she appeared as Lady Percy in *Henry IV* and Natella Aborshvilla in Brecht's *Caucasian Chalk Circle*.

Her television roles range from opera (*Dido and Aeneas*), Shakespeare (*Timon of Athens*) through popular drama (*C.A.T.S. Eyes*, *Dempsey and Makepeace*), to soap opera (she appeared as Apala in the *Brookside* spin-off *Damon and Debbie*).

Eventually the paths of the actress and the character of Norika Datta converged at Barlby Road. "The role of Norika Datta came about in a straightforward way - an interview followed by a screen test," says Seeta. "It was the first time I'd played a policewoman - and it was a question of jumping in at the deep end. I spoke to a number of officers to see what the work entailed. Perhaps the most difficult aspect was learning the various police procedures and getting accustomed to the constraints inherent to the job."

Among Seeta's favourite episodes

was 'CAD', written by JC Wilsher and directed by Christopher Hodson. "It was very concentrated and showed the tensions in the CAD Room when things go wrong."

And Norika has had her moments of high drama as a Beat officer. In Susan B. Shattock's 'Just for the Moment', directed by Tom Cotter, she was held at knife-point by a teenager who had been brought in to Sun Hill accused of stabbing his mother. The story also hinted at the mutual attraction between Datta and Jim Carver, although the expected romance did not blossom and a later episode would introduce us to Norika's boyfriend, Peter.

In 'The Chase', by Carole Harrison, directed by Stuart Urban, Norika rescued a baby left in a car during an armed robbery. And in 'Losing It', she was attacked by the psychologically disturbed Phil Young as they searched a warehouse together.

Seeta Indrani is a very private person who has successfully managed to maintain a low profile in what is generally regarded as the most 'high profile' profession of them all.

Vikki Gee-Dare came up through the 'walk-on' ranks to become a Sun Hill regular in the guise of the caring WPC, Suzanne Ford. "When I first worked on *The Bill*, in the hour-long episodes, I was also learning sign language with the ultimate intention of becoming an interpreter for the deaf - and the walk-on work fitted in well with my tuition," she explained.

Vicki Gee-Dare

At that time the signing obviously took precedence in Vikki's life. She had initially decided to study the language after watching an interpreter on television. "It looked so expressive, I loved the flowing movement of the hands. I went on a beginners' course at the City Literary Institute's Centre for the Deaf and was hooked immediately - it was as though a whole new world had opened up.

"You are taught by deaf teachers while training, but there comes a time when you have to try it in the outside world. I first took the plunge in a cafe in Broadstairs. I saw two girls signing then introduced myself to them with my hands trembling. Fortunately they were very kind and we've since become great friends."

Vikki later progressed through the intermediate and advanced stages of her tuition, and can now work as an interpreter.

And she was able to combine her signing skills with her acting career. "I interpreted for a special performance of *American Eagle* at the Lyric Theatre, Hammersmith - a two hour play in which I had to sign the parts of all the comic-type characters ranging from a mad professor to a super hero and it therefore required a lot of additional expressive body movement. It was great fun to do."

Vikki also interpreted the childrens' show *The Pied Piper* at the National Theatre and appeared as Lydia, the partially-hearing girl in *Children of a Lesser God* in Westcliff, along with the profoundly deaf actress Jean St Claire who understudied Elizabeth Quinn in the famous West End production.

Vikki - who had also worked on TV in *The Two Ronnies*, *The Duchess of Duke Street*, *The Little Mermaid*, and *This Happy Breed* - originally came to *The Bill* expecting to work only for a single day. "But I must have fitted the uniform, because they kept asking me back and I became a regular walk-on - one of those faces you see in the background representing the other Sun Hill staff."

Much to her surprise, she began to get fan mail asking why she wasn't more involved in the stories. And, in 1989, when the producers were looking for a new WPC, several people in the cast and the production team suggested that they audition Vikki. "That was very reasurring," she said. "I did a reading and Bob's-your-Uncle."

Suzanne Ford has been described as

'the ideal WPC'. She considered becoming a nurse before eventually joining the Metropolitan Police and she sees her policing role as essentially one of serving the community rather than catching crooks. "She's a natural copper," says Vikki. "And she's 'one of the boys' who always seems to get sent out on raids - but above all she is a caring woman. And of course, she knows sign language because she has a profoundly deaf sister."

After work one day Vikki was enjoying a drink with a deaf friend in a pub near the Sun Hill HQ. "We were talking (signing), when the scriptwriter Patrick Harkins spotted us. We got talking about sign language and our conversation ultimately led to his writing an episode called '*Watch My Lips*', for which I was made script consultant and interpreter at the auditions for deaf actors." In the episode WPC Ford used her signing skills to question a deaf suspect played by Tony Newton.

Vikki Gee-Dare was born in Lewisham, south-east London, but she spent the early years of her life in Singapore. "For most of my life I was the only child in a single-parent family - my father died when I was very young," said Vikki. "My mother was attached to the RAF as a teacher and when the opportunity arose to go East, she picked me up and off we went. We stayed in Singapore for three-and-a-half years and then came back to Ladywell, where I went to junior school."

But a lot more travelling was to come for Vikki as her mother's work took them all over the country. "My education came from many schools," she recalls.

And she still travels whenever she can, one of her recent trips being to Israel where, inspired by Mark Wingett's example, she learned to scuba dive. "I went down to thirty metres - it

was marvellous, like being suspended in space. And, guess what? I even taught the instructors some sign language for use underwater."

Delia French was once in charge of the typing pool at Sun Hill (although she was then known as Delia France). And, as Tosh Lines will testify, she was a proper slave driver. In '*Don't Like Mondays*', she balled him out for the generally sloppy quality of the CID tapes presented to her girls for audio-typing.

Natasha Williams

"That was a nice part for me," says Jamaican-born Natasha Williams. "I thought, this will make a good entry on my CV, and that was it as far as I was concerned. But they must have liked my work, because I was called back months later for a regular part."

Bossy Delia had left Sun Hill to work in a clerical job in the city. But that didn't suit her either, and she decided to return to police work, eventually becoming a Probationary WPC at Sun Hill. "That's the thing about Delia," says Natasha, "she thinks she can do anything - and she's so enthusiastic, she puts herself forward for things."

And that's precisely what Natasha did when she first decided to become an actress.

"We came over from Jamaica to live in Stafford when I was a little girl," she said. "We arrived in winter, just before Christmas - I'd never been so cold before. But I loved going to primary school here. I'd been to school in Jamaica but there were no blackboards or books, we'd just sat on the floor and listened. Now, with Christmas' coming they put up those coloured crepe paper decorations and there was a nativity play - I thought it was all magic.

"A few years later, at another school, a music teacher wrote a play about Emmeline Pankhurst. When they asked for a volunteer to play the lead, I pushed myself to the front - I had no idea who Emmeline Pankhurst was, never mind that she was white - I just wanted to do it. But they told me to get to the back of the class. Later still, when it came time to decide on a career, I said I wanted to be an actress and they told me to forget it."

Undaunted, Natasha did her first "proper" acting at college and later applied for an audition at the Royal Academy of Dramatic Art. "For my Shakespeare piece I gave them Juliet's dying speech. Very sad, very moving. As I was acting my heart out, I thought they were just holding themselves together. Tears were trickling down their cheeks. Then, as the scene came to its end, I saw that their bodies were shaking - with laughter. RADA told me to think long and hard before embarking on a theatrical career."

Eventually Natasha did get into a drama school, the Webber-Douglas Academy, a three year course beginning in 1982. But she left with two terms still to run. "I just couldn't hack it any more," she said. "Especially when someone told me that being black meant the only parts I'd ever play were maids. I didn't write any letters, or make any phone calls like you're supposed to do. But then I began to get calls, people had remembered me from certain drama school productions. I

and I wrote a lot of my own stuff which was incorporated into the show."

More theatre work followed for Natasha in Liverpool, Sheffield and London. She also appeared in a number of TV productions including episodes of *London's Burning* and *Brookside* and the BBC series *Fighting Back*, with Hazel O'Connor and, of course, as bossy Delia of the *Sun Hill* typing pool - all of which were interspersed with further spells of nannying.

Now Delia French is a firmly established character in *The Bill* and the girl who was once told to 'forget it' has made it as an actress.

"Delia had a great start on the beat," says Natasha, "She caught a villain purely by accident while being 'puppy walked' by Sergeant Peters in Chris Russell's '*Off the Leash*'. Since then she's shown that she likes being with the men - it doesn't bother her if she's the only woman in the pub - she can be just as disgusting as they are.

"I think it's very important that she reflects the Met's need to recruit more black officers. And she is generally enjoyed by black viewers, perhaps because she's so bubbly. Black policewomen in particular seem really pleased when they see me.

"Delia and I are both determined to make the most out of life. We're both going to make sure we have a good innings - just like the West Indies cricket team."

And if Delia French had her way, she would probably be running Sun Hill by now.

then went to about twenty interviews, but didn't get a single job. I thought, that's it, I've done my best - now I'll go and become a full-time nanny, something I'd done a lot of ... or a female Lenny Henry!"

Finally, a theatre group called Resister invited Natasha to join them. "Great, I thought, a nice ethnic group, sounds good to me. But they were feminists - and although I knew who Emmeline Pankhurst was by then, I didn't really know too much about feminist issues. I was frightened to death. But it was great and I soon learned about those issues and got seriously involved with them. We did a workshop about battered women, mentally battered, physically battered,

Despite his increasing popularity as Sun Hill's George Garfield, Huw Higginson is a young man with his feet firmly on the ground and a realistic approach to his chosen profession.

"I come from a theatrical family and know all about the good times and the bad times in acting," he says. "And I've still got lots of friends who I've known ever since junior school in Teddington - so when I'm with them there's no chance of my becoming big-headed. I'm just one of the lads."

Huw Higginson

Huw was born in Wrexham, north Wales, on 21 February 1964. When his father, Tim Wilton, joined the Royal Shakespeare Company the family moved to Stratford-on-Avon for a while. Huw's mother was an actress, but has since become an agent. His parents later divorced and he now has a stepfather, Roger Walker, who is also an actor. "And I recently went to see my sister, Emma Higginson, in her professional acting debut - so we really are a theatrical family."

The family settled in Teddington when Huw was eight years old. He still lives there, in a flat which he shares with his girlfriend. He went to school in Ham, on the opposite bank of the Thames.

As a twelve-year-old he appeared on the stage of the RSC, alongside his father in *Henry IV, Part II*. "I played Falstaff's page. It was great. I was quite fearless and started stealing laughs during the soliloquy, for which I was constantly ticked-off."

After that experience Huw knew he wanted to be an actor. "But my folks were dead set against the idea. They wanted me to go to university."

Instead he decided to take a year off before making a decision. In that time he did fourteen jobs ranging from scaffolder's mate to encyclopaedia salesman. "The only one I was any good at was the scaffolding, even though I hate heights."

After twelve months Huw was convinced that nothing, other than acting, had managed to capture his interest. "Going through all those jobs really reinforced my feelings about it - so I applied to drama schools and was accepted first time round at the London Academy of Dramatic Art, on a three years course between 1983 and 1986. I had a good time at LAMDA, although there's only so much a drama school can teach you. Acting is about trusting your instincts as much as anything else."

Having been offered a contract in Westcliff which would ensure his Equity ticket, Huw left LAMDA with two terms left to run. But, frustratingly he was simultaneously offered the chance of a TV role in Geoff McQueen's *Big Deal* "I couldn't do it. However, I later got another part in one episode of the TV serial - as a villainous biker."

Soon after this Huw was interviewed for a regular role in *The Bill*. " I've no idea which part it was, but nothing came of it." He returned to LAMDA for the last two weeks of the course and to appear in the annual musical production there. Then came a nationwide tour in *The Dawn*

59

Treader, followed by a job at the Library Theatre, Manchester.

In 1988 he appeared in several TV commercials and a number of training films and also landed a plum role as an English villain with a talent for American football in the BBC film *Defrosting the Fridge*, scripted by Ray Connelly. "Then, just just after Chistmas I was called in again by *The Bill*. And ater five interviews, I was eventually offered a twelve episode contract as PC George Garfield. I was given a line here and a line there - I suppose they were seeing what I was like - and they eventually decided to keep me on."

George Garfield arrived at Sun Hill, having spent a couple of years on the Teddington (!) manor and as a result of his constant requests to be transferred to a more urban environment. "George is an honest lad," says Huw. "And he has a sound integrity. He's had a couple of run-ins with Dave Quinnan, because he doesn't really approve of rule bending."

Unfortunately, Garfield also has a tendency to behave like the proverbial bull in a china shop. "There's a lot of humour attached to those aspects of his character - and I enjoy that - I love comedy, it's probably what I do best. And though *The Bill* is true to life drama, there is always humour in reality."

And will George Garfield progress in the Force? "He works hard and he's keen and willing," says Huw. "But he'll never go any higher than Sergeant because he's not really bright enough."

Like Garfield, Huw has always been a keen sportsman. "I did a bit of boxing as a schoolboy but was nowhere near George's level - he reached ABA quarter-final standard. I used to play rugby, but these days my main sporting enjoyment comes from playing cricket." And it was in the cricketing whites of *The Bill* Charity XI that Huw enjoyed a glorious innings against William Franklyn's Celebrity XI. "I faced up to John Snow - the ex-England opening bowler (202 Test wickets) and was pleasantly surprised when I knocked his first ball along the ground for a four. I was eventually 110 not-out and we won by three runs."

Huw Higginson looks set for along innings in *The Bill*.

Andrew Mackintosh could hardly believe his luck when, in the summer of 1988, he heard that *The Bill* were attempting to cast a twenty-eight year-old, clarinet playing, Scottish Detective Sergeant.

"I was working as the musical director of a show in Plymouth at the time," says Andrew. "I had just turned twenty-eight, I'd lived in Scotland as a boy and therefore had a Scottish accent, I played reed

Andrew Mackintosh

instruments, including clarinet, and I'd been an actor/musician since leaving drama school. So, I called *The Bill* casting department and was invited for an interview at Barlby Road."

Andrew made the journey from Devon to London, thinking there could not be many twenty-eight-year-old-Scottish-clarinet-playing-actors around. "Which just goes to show how wrong you can be. I met two of them at the interview, never mind those they'd already seen," he recalls.

But the interview went well. Andrew demonstrated his considerable musical skills and displayed exactly the right temperament for Alistair Greig.

"Greig's music was an important element of the characterisation to begin with. He was a keen amateur jazz player and he'd been a member of the Metropolitan Police Band. But there's only so much clarinet playing you can actually do in a cop show, so that side of his persona rather fell by the wayside."

At first Alistair Grieg was a mildly amusing character, with that particularly dry Scottish sense of humour. "I thought he was quite jolly to start with, but beneath that seemingly mild exterior lies a real tough cookie. He's incredibly ambitious and knows exactly where he's going - he came in on the Graduate Training Scheme and will probably go on to become a DI, or even a DCI. And he'll do it all by-the-book."

Unlike DI Burnside and DS Roach, Alistair Grieg also fits comfortably into the modern mode of policing, with its change of emphasis towards a management mentality. "Burnside and Roach are more of the old school, whereas Grieg takes a more intelluctual stance and is quite happy to work under the the stronger constraints now prevalent in the force. And that, of course, makes for some terrific conflicts, particularly with Burnside.

"I really enjoy playing Alistair Grieg. And it's not just to do with the high standards set on *The Bill*; it's also to do with the friendly atmosphere here at 'Sun Hill'. We all get on tremedously well together."

Andrew Mackintosh is a much-travelled man. He was actually born in Pennsylvania, USA, in August 1960. His parents had emigrated to The States in the late-50s; his father working in the electronics sector. "It means that my sister and I are both entitled to US citizenship, and she now lives in Washington DC," says Andrew. "We

eventually returned to England and then my father's work took us to Anstruther in Scotland when I was five."

It was during his schooldays in Scotland that Andrew's musical talents began to flourish, and when he joined a small drama group his twin ambitions were formed - to succeed at music and acting. For two years he read English and drama at Bristol University before leaving in 1981 to attend the Webber-Douglas drama school in London.

His first professional work was "...a mucking-in job with Jill Freud's company (Clement Freud's wife). We took a Christmas show around various town halls and everbody had to help out with everything. I loved it." Andrew's next engagement took him to Austria for eight months during which he earned his all-important Equity card. Next stop was the Everyman Theatre in Liverpool. "I went for just one job but ended up staying there, working as an actor and a musical director on several productions. The Everyman is a wonderful theatre and Liverpool is a wonderful city. I met my wife, Lucy, there - we now have a beautiful daughter, Melissa, and another child on the way."

Other theatre work followed for Andrew, mainly in the north-west and there was the occasional television role. "I played a sympathetic music teacher in *Every Breath You Take*, with Connie Booth and Brian Protheroe. But the most memorable of these tiny parts was that of an estate agent in *Coronation Street*. I worked for all of one morning with the splendid Jean Alexander who played Hilda Ogden. My character failed to interest her in a particular house."

And will Alistair Grieg ever dust off his clarinet in another epsiode of *The Bill*? "Who knows?" says Andrew. "Although he's hardly likely to become a 'Sherlock Holmes-musing-over-his-violin-type-character'. But perhaps I'll form a Bill Band for our Christmas party. Larry Dann is a very good piano player and Tom Butcher plays drums very well, and there's a lot more musical talent lurking around Sun Hill..."

Jeff Stewart was walking through Sloane Square, not far from his home in Chelsea, when a man in a smart Burberry raincoat, complete with upturned collar, sidled up to him. "He was obviously an off-duty policeman," says Jeff. "And he muttered under his breath, ' 'Ollis, if you was my Collator, I'd 'ave you bleedin' shot', and then he walked on again. As an actor, I took it as a great compliment."

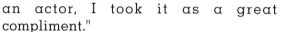

Jeff Stewart

Indeed, so convincing is Jeff Stewart's portrayal of Sun Hill's resident whinger, Reg Hollis, that even Brian Hart the show's hard-boiled Police Advisor praises the creation. "I definitely recognise him. There's been a Hollis-type in every station I've worked in," said Brian. "I've heard that whiney, whiney voice so many times before - I reckon he's one of the best drawn characters in *The Bill*."

Yet Reg Hollis, alias Jeff Stewart, almost didn't make it into the programme. "In the spring of 1984 my agent sent me along to the Thames studios at Teddington where they were casting for *The Bill*," said Jeff. "I met Peter Cregeen and we spoke for half an hour or so. He ended the conversation by saying that unfortunately I didn't fit any of the character descriptions. But as I was leaving, he called me back and stood there pondering. Then we talked for another ten minutes - he felt that I definitely had something to offer *The Bill*, eventually promised me a job in just one episode. It would be the first

acting work I'd done in eight months."

The episode was duly shot and Jeff went off to find more work. Three weeks later another large envelope bearing the Thames TV logo flopped through his letterbox. "I didn't open it, thinking it must have been sent to me by mistake. I called my agent, she called Thames and then got back to me saying I was to open it - it was a new Bill script."

Jeff appeared in no less than seven episodes in the first series, ten in the second series, in which Reg Hollis became Sun Hill's Collator - and he's now a permanent fixture at Sun Hill.

Jeff was born in Aberdeen, in October 1955, but spent his childhood in various parts of Hampshire. As a three-year-old, Jeff won a certificate in a schools' acting competition - for his expertly mimed interpretation of a fish.

He went to college to study the history of art. "I wasn't the best of students and hardly put pen to paper in two years," he remembers. "I did all my art in a week and got surprisingly good exam results. Then I went out into the big wide world and found a job operating a video camera."

Jeff was then accepted at a north London drama school, on a three year course. "I'd been there about six weeks when the novelty wore off, I got bored by it all, and when I nodded off during a class. I realised it was time to move on and try to get my Equity card by other means. Everyone in the class thought I was mad."

The next development in Jeff Stewart's career was most definitely one of those instances of 'being in the right place at the right time'. The place was a pub in the heart of London's theatreland. The time, two weeks later, coincided with the non-arrival of an assistant stage manager at the nearby Cambridge Theatre during the run of the musical *Ipi Tombi*. "I was having a drink at the bar and got into conversation with a rather harrassed looking couple who turned out to be the stage manager and company manager at the Cambridge. One of their ASM's had let them down for the umpteenth time and they were tearing their hair out looking for a replacement..."

A year later Jeff Stewart was the proud possessor of an Equity card. He alternated theatre work with appearances in a number of stout and lager ads before landing a plum role as a Scotsman in *The Nightmare Man* on TV. Other TV work followed, in *Crossroads*, *Minder*, *Give Us a Break*, *Help* and *Hi de Hi*. "I was Harry Fellows in *Crossroads*, a nasty piece of work, who driving a

Cortina, knocked down Benny, putting him in hospital for a while. About a year later I received a cheque for £14 - it was a repeat fee - Benny had apparently remembered the accident in a dream sequence."

But as 1984 got underway Jeff Stewart was beginning to believe that he would never work again.

The Bill changed all that. "Reg Hollis is a gift, an actor's dream," confirms Jeff. "He is funny without knowing it. He's enthusiastic, but his enthusiasm bubbles up in some funny places. He was chuffed in Kevin Clarke's '*Skeletons*' when he found what might have been the remains of a mass murder. And, as Burnside remarked 'there's definitley something unhealthy about you, Hollis'. Getting the part was great. Getting the series was even better, and when it turned into a half-hour show, twice a week for fifty-two weeks in the year - it was the fulfilment of a fantasy I'd had as a child: I'd always wondered what it would be like to appear in a long running TV series..."

'I'm very proud of 'Tosh'. He's a good lad," says Kevin Lloyd. "He's streetwise and has a copper's nose, an instinct which rarely fails him. I played cricket with a CID team recently and they asked if I'd come to work with them because Tosh seems to solve every case he's involved with. I said I'd love to join them, but I'd need a good scriptwriter along every time."

DC Alfred 'Tosh' Lines has indeed featured in some terrific episodes of *The Bill*. One that Kevin particularly enjoyed was '*Black Monday*', written by PJ Hammond, and directed by Alan Bell. "Tosh's ancient Volvo had broken down yet again on the way to work, so he got on a bus and saw someone who had reportedly committed suicide years ago, when he was nicked for a banking fraud on Tosh's previous patch in Essex.

"The lads in the office think he's cracking up, they can't see why he's bothering to rake over the past. But of course tenacious Tosh isn't cracking up at all. He's simply got the bit between his teeth and he won't let go - and it turns out that he's absolutely right. The man had re-appeared in the Sun Hill area, as the chief accountant in a building society. It was a smashing story and it summed up Tosh perfectly."

Before joining the cast of *The Bill* in August 1988, Kevin Lloyd was already a vastly experienced stage and screen actor. In 1975 he was nominated as 'Best

Kevin Lloyd

Newcomer' for his performance in Lindsay Anderson's production of Joe Orton's *What The Butler Saw*, at London's Royal Court Theatre. Among his most memorable TV roles were those of Harry Blackburn, the plumber with country & western leanings, in *Auf Wiedersehen Pet* and Ricky Fortune, the fading pop star in *Dear John*. "That was a lovely part and although Ricky only appeared in two episodes, he became an instant hit with the public. My wife Lesley and I were in Nottingham once when a group of rugby players serenaded us with every verse of Ricky's song '*Not On My Birthday*'. The writer John Sullivan did consider giving Ricky his own serial, but nothing ever came of it. I think he went off to reform his old group, 'cause I've never heard from him since. The episode was shown again recently when the BBC re-ran *Dear John* as a tribute to the late Ralph Bates who was so brilliant in the title role."

Kevin was a natural choice for the part of Alfred 'Tosh' Lines. He was born in Derby in 1949, the son of a Detective Sergeant policeman who died in a road accident while rushing to what turned out to be a false-alarm when Kevin was twenty-one. "My uncle and my grandfather were also policemen and I was, of course, brought up in a police house - so I have many memories to draw upon when I'm playing Tosh Lines."

And, like Tosh, Kevin has a large family of his own (James, Poppy and

Henry have played his children in *The Bill*). "He has five children, I have six - facts which did lead to a little confusion during one episode, in which Chris Ellison had to deliver a line relating to Tosh's five children. But because Chris knows me so well, he got real life and fiction mixed up and said that Tosh had six kids. The episode was duly broadcast and no one noticed the slip until those keen-eyed *Sierra Oscar* girls pointed it out in the fanzine."

The Lloyd household, in Derbyshire, was increased by one in the autumn of 1991 when Kevin and Lesley completed the adoption of a Romanian baby. "My good friend Stuart Webb is the managing director of my favourite football club, Derby County, in which I'm also a shareholder. His wife, Josie, is involved with TREATS, a charity whose aim is simply to give 'treats' to under-privileged children. When the Romanian revolution happened, they decided to do everything they could for all those unwanted children."

Lesley Lloyd joined the committee and

helped launch the TREATS/Derby Evening Telegraph Appeal for Romanian Children in the autumn of 1990. She travelled to Romania three times helping to deliver vital supplies. Each time she returned distraught and heartbroken.

"On Lesley's fourth trip, to Timosoara in February 1991, I went with her. I saw an overcrowded children's home where boys were crammed in fifty to a room; I saw a hospital with two babies to an incubator; I saw the deformed children - a result of their mothers taking drugs to get rid of them when abortion was banned."

There and then, the Lloyds decided to adopt a Romanian child. They were taken to a hospital in Hunendora to see three newly-born abandoned babies. It was an agonising choice, to have to leave two behind, but they eventually settled on a little girl called Eleanora.

"Back home, we held a family conference around the kitchen table," says Kevin. "If any of the children had any doubts whatsoever we would call it off. But they were all for it, I was proud of them. My youngest, Edward, calls her 'Baby Norna'. He feels quite big now because he's no longer the littlest.

"We sorted out the adoption proceedings in England and in May we returned to Romania to appear before a Judge and to meet the real mother who had to formally agree to the adoption."

By then the baby was four months old and, incredibly, had been kept constantly in a tiny room. "We took her out into the fresh air for the first time in her life," says Kevin. "Her face lit up as she felt the breeze on her face and in her hair. She was seeing green grass for the first time - I recorded these magical moments on videotape to show her when she gets older. We spent the week with her and then went home to wait for all that interminable paperwork to go through. Now she is ours."

In his first television role, Tom Butcher played a policeman in *Coronation Street*. "It was just a day's work in 1988," said Tom. "They put me in the blue serge uniform, gave me a notebook and stood me between 'Bet and Alec Gilroy' - Julie Goodyear and Roy Barraclough. I had to take a statement from Alec who claimed he had been mugged and robbed of the weekend's takings on his way to the bank. I was pretty nervous. It was quite a daunting experience - and that notebook seemed to be shaking a lot on screen."

Tom's second television role was also as a policeman, but this time the assignment lasted a lot longer than a day.

"I came along to *The Bill* at a time when several actors in the programme were coming to the end of their contracts, and it had been decided to introduce a few more 'regional' coppers into the Sun Hill personnel. It was a case of right face, right desk, right time," he claims modestly.

But there was obviously a lot more to winning the role than simple coincidence. Many actors were interviewed and auditioned and Tom was called back several times before he eventually donned the uniform of the hard young Mancunian, Steve Loxton.

Although born in Stamford, Lincolnshire - the only boy among five

Tom Butcher

sisters - Tom had spent most of his student days in Manchester. "My father is a lawyer and I'd first considered a career in the law, then it was to be anthropology - but I finally settled on drama because I'd really enjoyed acting ever since playing Poins in *Henry IV*, at school. So, I studied drama at the Manchester Poly for three years, and went straight from there to the Edinburgh Festival with a company called Think Again, playing Shylock in Arnold Wesker's *Merchant*."

Other theatre work followed, mainly in the Manchester area and at some point along the way a friend suggested that Tom should write to *The Bill*'s casting department. "It took me about a year to get around to writing that letter," says Tom. "But it brought me to Sun Hill's attention and eventually I was called in..."

After a somewhat stormy and controversial period in which Tom went 'walkabout' in Australia, he has now returned to the fold and is now happy to be back in the blue serge of *The Bill*.

"Steve Loxton loves wearing the uniform and is always one of the best turned out coppers on the beat," said Tom. "He was originally perceived as the most unpopular PC in Sun Hill, but you can't avoid the fact that in times of crisis there is an inevitable closing of ranks, so no matter how unpopular someone is, he's still one of your

number. And as time has gone by Steve has gradually become more accepted."

Steve Loxton can turn on the charm when necessary, but is equally quick to switch it off again. He is certainly a selfish character, a manipulator who is out for what he can get. He even switched careers from the Army to the Police when he realised the force would give him a little more leeway, a little more independence.

Loxton is a qualified Area Car driver, a distinction he shares with Tony Stamp. And, being something of a natural show-off, he was unable to resist the opportunity - in Susan B. Shattock's 'Just for the Moment' - to demonstrate his driving skills in front of George Garfield and a group of football supporters, by excuting a spectacular U-turn and then racing off at high-speed.

But his real ambition is to become a firearms officer. "And maybe that will happen," says Tom. "He'll certainly be doing everything in his power to achieve it. He once said he doesn't

intend to end his days as 'Sun Hill's Plod'. It's exciting to watch him develop - I really enjoy playing Steve Loxton."

And the notebook doesn't shake any more.

In his previous posting, at a police station in North London, Sergeant John Maitland had shopped two of his fellow officers for drinking on duty. "I think he was right to do it," says Sam Miller, the Suffolk-born actor who portrays Maitland on screen. "They were traffic police and they were definitely out of order."

The subsequent air of mistrust surrounding Maitland made his presence at the station distinctly

Sam Miller

uncomfortable for all concerned, including himself. He had to move on - to Sun Hill, where his arrival was naturally viewed through wary eyes.

But Maitland is thick-skinned. He doesn't give a monkey's what others think of him. His very first relief at Sun Hill were reminded in no uncertain terms that he does not tolerate bent coppers or drinking on duty, but that he will back those who give 100 per cent all the way.

And he quickly won the grudging respect of his new colleagues by getting stuck in when Ted Roach was brutally attacked by a gang of thugs outside a pub. "He didn't hesitate," recalls Sam. "His size eleven boot was planted right between the legs of one thug, hard enough to make his eyes water."

Since then John Maitland has continued to stamp his authority on Sun Hill. "He leads from the front," says Sam. "Despite being a stickler for the rule book, he will invariably be the first in

there. And he would never ask anyone else to do something he isn't prepared to do himself. He has his faults, though, probably because he is such a relatively young Sergeant. He certainly lacks diplomacy and often plays it by the book perhaps a little too closely. He can be sensitive, particularly when dealing with the public, but his insensitive side often shows when he's working alongside experienced PCs. It's only when he makes personal relation-ships with people that he allows himself to be himself. It's an interesting role to play."

Sam Miller's route to Sun Hill was a lot less fraught than John Maitland's had been. He was born in the village of Saxmundham, Suffolk, in September 1962. After leaving school and college clutching a handful of 'A' levels, he and some friends formed a new wave band called The Push which became reasonably well-known in East Anglia.

"The Push gradually evolved into a kind of avant-garde cabaret act. It became more theatrical and I found that I really enjoyed that aspect of it. I'd always been a great fan of gangster films and had always harboured a secret ambition to be an actor. So, I decided it was time to give it a try. I had spells at the Maddermarket Theatre in Norwich and then enrolled at the Arts Educational Drama School in London."

By sheer coincidence Sam made his professional acting debut in Suffolk - in the musical, *Chicago*, at the Wolsey Theatre, Ipswich.

Other theatrical roles followed, including a year's run in the West End, in Shakespeare's *Richard II* and *Richard III*, and a season of alfresco Shakespeare at the Regent's Park Theatre.

Sam has also appeared in the TV films *Murder East- Murder West*, the first film to be shot in re-united Germany and *Great Escape - The Final Chapter*, with Christopher Reeves; and the series *Boon*, *Wish Me Luck*, *Van Der Valk*, *Casualty*, *Campion* and *A Piece of Cake*. He was first seen as John Maitland in *The Bill* in January 1991.

"Although I wasn't a regular viewer of the show, I'd always admired *The Bill* - especially its ability to deal with serious issues head-on".

Sam's most enjoyable episode to date

was the highly praised *'They Also Serve'*, written by Russell Lewis, directed by David Hayman and set almost entirely in the back of a police van at the scene of a demo.

"David insists on doing everything in long takes, which in itself is not unusual for *The Bill* - we often have lengthy scenes of action which help to give the programme its documentary look. But in this instance the entire first-half consisted of one take, fifteen minutes of real time, which is quite a departure. I think we did it about seven or eight times. The episode captured all the humour that comes out in any group of police officers in tense situations ."

Off screen, Sam Miller lives a hectic life. He shares a north London flat with a friend. He is a founder member of Raw Bread, a company which produces workshop performances of the works of new playwrights and introduces them to established theatres and producers.

He relaxes by playing golf or tinkering with one of the Volkswagen 'beetles' which he is painstakingly restoring. He keeps fit by riding his touring bike halfway across London to *The Bill* studios.

"Maitland is an efficient, ambitious, career-minded policeman," concludes Sam. "A high-flyer who is definitely on his way up the promotion ladder. But not too soon, I hope."

But when Sergeant Maitland does eventually move on, Sam Miller won't be too worried. "I want to develop as an actor - to play as many different and varied roles as possible. One I'd really like to tackle is the James Cagney role in a re-make of *White Heat* ('Made it, Ma - the top of the world, Ma!')."

Now that really would be a departure from the stolid Mr Maitland.

Cathy Marshall arrived at Sun Hill in a blaze of glory having just been awarded her commendation for bravery for single-handly arresting an armed robber on her previous manor.

"It was Cathy's own choice to become Sun Hill's Collator," says Lynne Miller. "Although it had been offered to her as a kind of protective gesture by the Met. And it was a very prestigious job in terms of the rapport the Collator has with the high ranks. Thankfully, she was written in quite strongly, so I had solid foundations on which to build the characterisation. It was a very comfortable way for me to join the series - and I've loved every minute of it

Lynne Miller

ever since."

Lynne was born in Guy's Hospital, just south of London Bridge "...and just about within the sound of Bow Bells - if you've got very good hearing".

She was brought up in south-east London along with her younger brother who is now a doctor. Their father worked as a general manager in various theatres. "He was involved with lots of musicals, which obviously meant I had a very early connection with the business," said Lynne. "And from the age of about twelve onwards there was no question that I wanted to do anything other than acting."

Lynne eventually went to university where she gained a degree in English and drama. Unusually, she made her

professional debut on television (rather than on stage) in the early '70s in a *Love Story* called '*Audrey Had a Little Lamb*'. Many more TV and theatre roles followed and in 1975 she won the Plays & Players Most Promising Actress Award, for her portrayal of Nicola Davis in Steven Poliakoff's *Hitting Town* and *City Sugar*, the second of which was a huge success in the West End. Lynne then joined the Old Vic Company and toured the UK and Australia with their productions of *Trelawny of the Wells* and *The Merchant of Venice*. She is married to a photographer and has one daughter, Jessica.

In the spring of 1989 she was invited along to Barlby Road to be considered for the role of Cathy Marshall in *The Bill*. "I had no idea whether I had the part or not and had put it to the back of my mind. A few days later, I was at a party when one of the programme's directors came over and congratulated me on my new job. It was a pleasant surprise, but I think he was worried that he'd given a secret away, because it hadn't yet been officially announced."

Cathy Marshall remained as Sun Hill's Collator for almost a year. But by then she was becoming frustrated with the job and its nine-to-five routine, and she asked to return to the beat. Urged on by Bob Cryer, who knew Cathy's talents were perhaps being wasted in the LIO office, Inspector Monroe reluctantly granted her request.

"I was quite pleased when that happened," said Lynne. "After all, there is a limit to the number of storylines that can be based around a filing system."

Cathy is basically soft-hearted, a condition well protected by her crisp manner and sharp sense of humour. She's a vastly experienced, solid and reliable policewoman. And she's a born organiser who can't understand why others aren't - a fact which has sometimes caused others to call her 'bossy'.

She has passed her Sergeant's exams and may one day move up the promotion ladder. On numerous occasions she has worn the two stripes denoting the rank of Acting Sergeant - most notably when she was put in temporary charge of the unruly 'C' Relief. "After a bit of a struggle she succeeded in stamping her authority on the relief, but then decided that the Sergeant's life was not really for her. I think at heart she loves pounding the beat."

She has also known some sadness in her life - she was once married to a CID officer, but divorce became inevitable when he began to beat her. She confessed this to to Viv Martella in '*Kidding*', written by Jonathan Rich. And in Russell Lewis's '*Forget Me Not*' her ex-husband, Clive, asked her for a reconciliation. She refused - and he was about to strike her when Quinnan intervened. Cathy then made it plain that she never wanted to see her ex-husband again.

In '*Near the Knuckle*', by Ayshe Raif, her GP was brought in to Sun Hill having allegedly assaulted his wife. Ironically, Cathy had consulted him when her husband had attacked her. Having seen him for what he is, she informed him that in future she would visit a different doctor.

"Her unfortunate personal experience makes her an ideal candidate for the domestic violence unit for which she has volunteered. She's a good listener," says Lynne. "And I'd say Cathy is a very responsible woman, without being pompous and boring about it. And you can bet she'll never go out with another policeman."

"If Trudie Goodwin had been dark haired, then I might never ever have made it to Sun Hill," says Nula Conwell. "It so happened that they needed a dark haired WPC to contrast with June Ackland and I fitted *The Bill*, so to speak. I was WPC 'X' and scheduled to appear in just one scene in an episode in the first series."

At that time Nula was also involved in other work. "I'd played the barmaid at 'Del Boy's' local in *Only Fools and Horses* and there was a possiblity of more work in that. I was also doing some public relations work for Prestel - I used to arrange photo-session and audition models for ads, and I helped out behind the scenes of the Bob Hope Golf Classic. I enjoyed the work and my manager there offered me a permanent management job - which my mother urged me to accept because it would be more secure than acting."

But while lunching with John Salthouse and others in the Thames canteen at Artichoke Hill she was offered another episode of *The Bill*. "'Has it got any lines?', I asked. 'No' they said. 'Give her some lines,' said John, and they finally agreed, so I accepted."

More episodes followed for Nula and WPC 'X' gradually evolved into WPC Viv Martella. "But I was still only contracted for short periods at a time throughout the first three series of *The Bill*, and

Nula Conwell

didn't become a 'regular' until the beginning of the half-hours."

By then WPC Viv was an integral member of Sun Hill's personnel. Although Nula didn't know it, she was heading for the CID office. "Whenever they needed a female officer to do plain clothes or undercover work, it would invariably fall to me or Trudie. And then I noticed that it was happening more for me and after a while I began to suspect that Viv might be in line for a transfer. I suppose it was always on the cards, since the programme had been running for so long without a female in CID."

Nula's suspicions were confirmed by Peter Cregeen when he called her in to discuss the situation. "He wanted to know if I was happy with the idea of Viv moving to CID, and of course I was delighted. It would be an interesting development for the character. And I was relieved at not having to wear that A-line skirt any more."

And so it was in a smart new suit that Viv Martella made her entrance in the CID office in 'One of the Boys', scripted by Jonathan Rich, directed by Alan Wareing. She had been in the job for a week and was already frustrated with the routine, hum-drum tasks to which she had been assigned by DI Burnside: we saw her typing a report while her CID colleagues discussed a Murder Squad investigation. Then Burnside told her she was 'too busy' to join the men in the pub at lunchtime to celebrate Dashwood's success in obtaining a conviction in another case. When she complained to Tosh Lines that she'd '...only been out for sandwiches and chips', he took pity and asked her to collect a local prostitute who was needed as a witness.

But it all went disastrously wrong. Martella lost the girl - twice - but by sheer persistence caught up with her and brought her in, only to discover that she was no longer needed for questioning. *En route* Viv had split the seams of her new suit and found herself being chatted up by a motorist who assisted her in the chase. Back at Sun Hill her CID colleagues poked fun at her bedraggled appearance, causing her to lose her temper with Burnside who reacted with a friendly 'welcome to the firm, Viv'.

"That was a lovely episode to mark her start in the CID office," says Nula. "Then came a natural period of settling in, of getting to know the ropes - for Viv and for me. She wasn't, for instance, sent out on jobs that only an experienced detective could handle. I actually discussed this with a real WDC and she said it took her a long while to establish herself and gain acceptance among her male CID colleagues."

104 episodes later in 'Double or Quits' written by Rib Davis, directed by Bill Pryde, Martella attempted to pull off, in court, one of Burnside's old tricks - namely the deliberate reading out, "by mistake", of a list of the prisoner's previous convictions. Such information is, of course, inadmissible since it is obviously prejudicial to the accused. "As it happens the ploy misfired," says Nula. "But the story showed that Viv had reached yet another stage in her development in that she now had the confidence to try the trick."

Viv Martella is young, attractive and single but she prefers to keep her social life entirely seperate from her work. And she will never become romantically linked with any of the men in the CID office. "When the idea of Viv's transfer was first discussed, I especially requested that she wouldn't have an affair with any of them. That smacked of the obvious to me. I felt it would make her no more than the token female in the office. Anyway an affair in that environment couldn't last and one of them would probably have to move on. I think it's far more interesting to explore, for instance, her genuine friendship with Tosh."

Nula is also opposed to the thought of too many tears trickling down Viv's cheeks. "I've had to fight quite a bit against the old idea that when a female is upset, she automatically bursts into floods of tears. I'm not saying women don't cry, of course they do, and I've gone

along with that in certain scenes. But on other occasions I've rebelled a bit.

"For instance, when Viv foolishly had a bit of a fling with someone who turned out to be a villain and then told Burnside all about it - I was originally supposed to weep throughout the whole scene. But really she hadn't done anything wrong and was really asking for Burnside's support and to be treated as an equal. Why would she cry in that situation? She might well do when she got home, but not in front of Burnside."

The scene was altered.

Nula is also involved in choosing Viv's wardrobe, in conjunction with the costume department. "We began by basing her clothing budget on a WDC's salary. Her clothes have to be practical as she does quite a lot of running around. She's a far more conservative dresser than I am and hardly ever wears jeans or trousers. I'm into lots of casual clothes and sportswear, she isn't and I'm

very glad about that - if we wore the same things, or shopped at the same shops, then I'd be living and breathing this job every single minute of the day."

Nula Conwell was born in Highbury, north London, the second of four daughters. Her parents are both Irish and her father, now retired, is a former lift engineer. She was brought up and educated in Islington, her interests at school gravitating towards the arts. And she went to the Anna Scher Children's Theatre in Islington.

"Anna was a school teacher who started up a kids' theatre club in a tiny hall. We were usually thrown out at 8 o'clock so the bingo could start. But I loved it there and made lots of friends, particularly Gillian Taylforth who plays Kathy in *EastEnders* and Andrew Paul who plays Dave Quinnan .

"Yet, I only went along because I loved doing drama," said Nula. "I never had any ambition to become an actress - it just sort of happened. When I was fifteen I was given a small part in a *Play for Today*, which was directed by the late Barry Davis. And when Barry went on to direct *Telford's Change*, with Peter Barkworth and Hanna Gordon in 1979, he gave me another small role, as a bank clerk, in seven episodes."

During the next four years, between jobs in hairdressing, catering and of course public relations, Nula appeared as a nurse in David Lynch's classic film *The Elephant Man*, and in several TV shows including *Only Fools and Horses*.

"Looking back, I realise that I was fortunate to be in three top quality productions. And that line has continued with *The Bill*. I'm glad I made the decision to accept that extra episode back in 1984. Things have gone really well - in fact, I couldn't be happier at work."

4 From Script to Screen

To produce 104 half-hour episodes of *The Bill* each year requires an operation of near military proportions. It's all achieved on a continuous cycle of planning meetings, technical rehearsals, and intensive shooting and editing sessions – all conducted under the watchful eye of 'The Boss', Executive Producer Michael Chapman.

Since the changeover to half-hourly episodes in 1988 *The Bill* has adopted a system which employs two seperate production teams – the Red Unit and the Blue Unit – each headed by a Producer and further divided into seperate teams all working on episodes at various stages of the production cycle.

Working simultaneously each Unit turns out two completed episodes every two weeks. Occasionally, if the reserve of episodes needs topping up, a Green Unit is created. "Things get pretty hectic when Red, Blue and Green are all operating at once," says Project Co-ordinator Nigel Wilson. "But believe me, there's a hell of a buzz around the place."

The Bill devours storylines like a hungry animal, and the Script Department are constantly looking for more tales with which to feed the beast. Inevitably the same themes crop up time and time again, yet one of the great strengths of *The Bill* lies in its in-built abilty to play endless variations on those themes. Similar subjects can provide completely different stories – a topic seen from a 'uniform' viewpoint for instance, will differ considerably when given a CID slant.

In the main, episode ideas come from the scriptwriters who initially write them up as a basic two or three paragraph premise. Sometimes a premise is initiated by the production unit, particularly when a character clash needs to be ironed out for the sake of future continuity. For instance, when Burnside and Roach had a serious punch-up in '*Caught Napping*', the writer, Russell Lewis, was specifically assigned to the task of bringing about a reconciliation and returning the relationship to its antagonistic norm.

Occasionally story ideas come from outside sources – even the police have been known to request that particular topics are covered (although that does not imply automatic acceptance).

All ideas are considered at the weekly script meeting, held each Wednesday and attended by Michael Chapman, Producers Tony

> Apart from network showing in Great Britain, *The Bill* is also a top-rated show in Australia and New Zealand. Episodes have also been transmitted in Bahrain, Barbados, Bulgaria, China, Dubai, Finland, Gibraltar, Greece, Holland, Hong Kong, Italy, Jamaica, Kenya, Malaysia, Mauritius, Norway, Republic of Ireland, Saudi Arabia, Singapore, Spain, Swaziland, Sweden, Thailand, Trinidad, USSR, Zambia and Zimbabwe.

The Bill's Police Advisor is Brian Hart, an ex-policeman of vast experience who spent most of his 31½ years of service at various stations in the East End of London, beginning as a Cadet in Plaistow and eventually rising to the rank of Chief Inspector. He was offered the job on *The Bill* when he retired from The Met in 1989. "I had always been a fan of *The Bill*," said Brian, "although I'd only been able to dip in and out of it as I was always involved with shift work. I'd been looking for an interesting challenge, and I grabbed the chance with both hands".

Throughout his working life Brian had known the police environment intimately, and the sudden switch to the world of television came as quite a shock. "It was a step into the unknown – but I'm glad I took it. And until 1990 I had the company of Wilf Knight, another ex-copper turned TV Police Advisor, who had been with *The Bill* since the beginning.

"My former rank of Chief Inspector (the same rank as Derek Conway) proved to be ideal for a Police Advisor as I'd had contact with the upper echelons of The Met and was still closely involved with the officers on the beat, and could therefore deal with queries at both ends of the spectrum."

Brian reads premises, storylines and scripts with an eye to the veracity of police procedures and attitudes. "If something is wrong, I'll always point it out. Hopefully, all errors have been ironed out when it comes to shooting an episode. We don't knowingly make something that is contrary to police practice. We endeavour to make our episodes as true to life as is humanly possible."

It is not only scriptwriters and script editors who come to Brian for advice. Directors and actors will often ask him to clarify a point of procedure in a script, and often a director will ask him to be on hand during the shooting of a particularly tricky piece of police business.

"I love the job," he says. "I'm proud to work on *The Bill*. I believe it reflects policemen as they really are – human beings coping with what is, at times, an extremely tough and stressful job."

Project Co-ordinator, Nigel Wilson

Virgo and Peter Wolfes, Script Editors Zanna Beswick and Gina Cronk, Assistant Script Editor Nicola Venning, Police Advisor Brian Hart and Project Co-ordinator Nigel Wilson. Every story premise is read and considered, essentially for dramatic content, procedural credibilty and the feasibility of shooting it on a five day schedule. A scriptwriter who submits a premise which is accepted as a potential episode is then asked to expand it into a three page storyline.

The team also discuss ideas which have already reached the storyline stage. If they still look promising, then a full script is commissioned from the writer.

Writers are obliged to research their material in depth. This often means visits to police stations, courts, hospitals, or social service establishments and asking questions pertinent to the subject of the episode. Writers (and cast members) can also attend a 'police interrogation course' in which they pose as suspects – 'innocent' or 'guilty' – under interrogation by real police officers.

"The police are very helpful," says Nigel Wilson. "It's a reciprocal thing – we are a fictional drama, they are a disciplined service. Both sides realise and accept this. Things run smoothly between us. I'd say our relationship with the Met is now as close as it could be, and as close as it should be."

When a batch of six scripts reach their first draft stage, they are 'packed' for either the Red or Blue unit. At this point each script is 'sponsored' by either of the two Producers. In turn, they will have assigned a Director to each episode (Directors usually work on two episodes in a batch). Nigel then breaks the scripts down individually, into their various components: cast requirements, locations, scenes inside Sun Hill etc. Having completed this exercise on each script he then matches them up to find pairs that could feasibly be recorded simultaneously.

"I have to take various factors into account," he said. "For example, an actor who features heavily in the Red Unit script could not appear too frequently in the Blue Unit story. Similarly, we couldn't have both Units shooting in the same part of Sun Hill at the same time, although we often have one working on the ground floor and the other upstairs."

Nigel next issues a 'guide track' which shows the feasibilty of the pairings and spells out any cast transfers that would be required between Units. This plan is distributed among the various department heads who each consider any further problems that might arise. "The system is designed to be as efficient and as flexible as possible. Any number of factors can alter it – for instance, the non-availability of a certain location on a particular day would change the plan. Or a change of characters might be required to make the pairing work more smoothly, and that could mean the revision of dialogue."

Eventually, with a few inevitable adjustments, all departments agree the 'guide track' and it evolves into a schedule for shooting, the next step towards eventual recording.

Meanwhile, other wheels are turning:

The Location Managers of each Unit begin to search for suitable locations called for by the scripts. This is done in close co-operation with an episode's Designer and Director, who will already have his or her own idea of how the finished product should look.

The Casting Department, also working closely with the Producer and Director, have begun looking for actors to fill all the non-regular roles, from featured villains, victims and witnesses to walk-on extras and stunt doubles.

The Costume Department will plan for the number of uniforms required on each shoot, as well as the CID suits and the clothing of all the other characters. The Make-up Department will prepare for the normal make-up and hairstyling that is an essential part of any television drama production. The script will also indicate any special make-up effects required, such as cuts, scars and bruises or more serious gunshot or knife wounds.

The Property Buyers and Stage Managers work closely together,

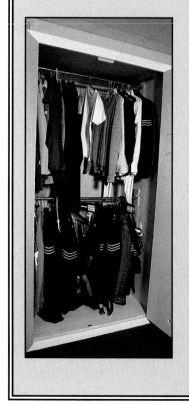

The Bill's uniforms are kept under lock and key for obvious security reasons, and no uniform is hung complete in the same cupboard.

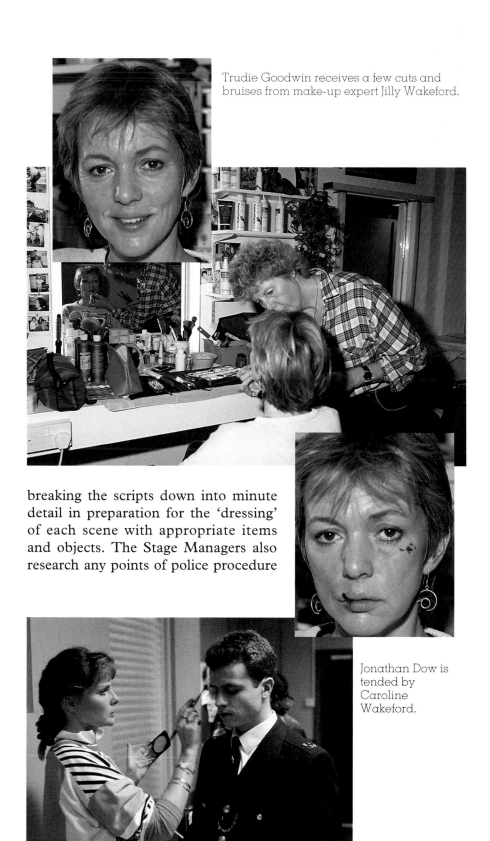

Trudie Goodwin receives a few cuts and bruises from make-up expert Jilly Wakeford.

breaking the scripts down into minute detail in preparation for the 'dressing' of each scene with appropriate items and objects. The Stage Managers also research any points of police procedure

Jonathan Dow is tended by Caroline Wakeford.

79

indicated in a script. In this way, should the Police Advisor be unavailable during the shoot, the Stage Manager becomes the final arbiter on any tricky procedural problems.

A technical 'recce' takes place on the Monday before a Director is due to begin shooting his episodes. The Director, Cameraman, Sound Supervisor and Lighting Director, together with the Stage Manager and the Director's First Assistant visit each location to fine tune the logistics of the shoot and iron out any potential time wasting problems. They may, for instance, decide that certain shots will require special equipment, such as a camera crane or a specialised lighting system.

Eventually, after many weeks of meticulous preparation, everything is ready for the Units' first five-day shoot. Working to a shooting schedule planned by Nigel Wilson, in conjunction with the Producers, Production Managers, Directors and their First Assistants, Red and Blue swing into action. Under the creative control of the Director, a crew aims to record around five minutes of screen time per day. They use the splendid lightweight M2 Ikegami camera system which records on half-inch tape – while naturalistic sound and as little lighting as possible, helps to maintain the sense of realism which is such an essential part of *The Bill*'s appeal.

By now the cast are well aware of the story and their part in it – although Sun Hill regulars tend not to learn their lines as thoroughly as they would for a theatrical production or a more conventional TV play. An Assistant Stage Manager is on hand at all times during the shoot, for any line rehearsals – particularly important for scenes involving non-regular artistes. Before a scene is recorded there is a brief rehearsal period on set, to block out movements in relation to the camera, but the essence of *The Bill*'s acting style lies in the spontaneous and fresh delivery of dialogue, *on camera*.

Several camera crews work on *The Bill*. In 1990 three of the camera team, Rolie Lukes, Roy Easton and Adrian J Fearnley won a Bafta Craft Award.

Jim Goddard (seated) is one of the many directors who work on the series.

Invariably certain cast members will be required to transfer between Units, to act in scenes in both episodes. Although the system is designed to avoid too many transfers, it sometimes happens that for various reasons actors can find themselves working on more than two stories at once. The current record is held by Peter Ellis who, on one occasion in 1989, worked on five different episodes in the same week.

(Above) The crew review a "take" on a video monitor.

(Below) One of The Bill's two specially built editing suites.

'Rushes' are viewed each evening and, as shooting progresses throughout the week, the Video Tape Editor assembles a rough cut of the episode in one of two purpose-built editing suites at the 'Sun Hill' base.

In general, episodes are successfully recorded within their allotted five days, but delays sometimes occur due to bad weather or technical problems. Occasionally the re-shooting of a scene is necessary and will be done as soon as possible after the main shoot, to prevent any delay in editing.

In two weeks, when the Director has completed his shooting schedule, he will sit down with the VT Editor and the Producer to see his episodes through the post production stage. At this point a story is edited to precisely 24 minutes and 35 seconds with a break at a suitably dramatic moment in the middle, in which to slot the obligatory, all-important commercials. Any extra dubbing is also done at this stage –

All re-shoots are colour-coded 'Beige', thereby giving an innocuous and perfectly innocent colour an unwarranted reputation within *The Bill's* headquarters. Comments like "You're looking a bit beige today" and "We've gone beige!" are often heard around Sun Hill. The inevitable 'out-takes' which lead to a beige status are painstakingly collected by the VTR Editors and the best – or perhaps the worst and most embarrassing – among them are re-edited together for showing at *The Bill's* annual cast and crew Christmas party.

For the 1990 party several of these hilarious "bloops, bleeps and blunders" were strung together and interspersed with Jon Iles' spot-on impersonation – splendidly directed by Larry Dann – of Dennis Norden hosting *It'll Be Alright On The Night*. On this evidence, those most guilty of the crime of 'corpsing', or giggling on camera, were the high-ranking Peter Ellis and Ben Roberts (Brownlow and Conway).

the addition of any incidental sounds or voice-overs, such as a beat officer's message coming into the CAD room via a personal radio. In general the post-production process takes no more than two weeks.

As with virtually all other elements in the production cycle, *The Bill's* transmission schedule is also extremely flexible. An episode can be recorded, edited and broadcast within a month, although the normal time span for transmissions is between three weeks and three months.

As the transmission date approaches, *The Bill's* Unit Publicist, Wendy Tayler, will have initiated the circulation of brief 'teasers' and stills of each episode (taken in the main by photographer Stan Allen

who took most of the pictures featured in this book) to all the newspapers and TV listings magazines, so that potential viewers will have a tantalising idea of what's in store at Sun Hill.

Finally, the most important factor of all comes into play when *The Bill*'s regular viewers, an estimated 12,000,000 to 13,000,000 in Britain, settle in front of their TV sets ready for the latest chapter in the Sun Hill casebook. If they like what they see, they will tune into the next episode – and the beat will go on, and on.

Just as storylines are devoured by the programme, so too are non-regular characters – and it's said that whenever three members of Equity, the actor's union, get together, two of them will inevitably be talking about their episodes in *The Bill*.

Although Casting Directors Pat O'Connell and Linda Butcher (plus a number of free-lance casting directors) are involved with the casting of any new principal characters their day-to-day work consists of filling all the non-regular roles. "The bigger, juicier parts are the easist to cast – it's the smaller, incidental roles that are difficult: 'Thug 1' and 'Thug 2', 'Attendants 1 and 2', or 'Traffic Cops 1,2,3 and 4' –

these types come up so often. Some actors are used quite often. For instance, a 'morose neighbour' might turn up several episodes later as 'irate man at bus stop'.

Between 5 April 1989 and 16 June 1991 the Casting Department filled no less than 17,878 walk-on parts, cast 3,643 non-regular roles and booked 260 stunts.

All stunts and fights are carefully staged by experts, to prevent accidents. Here, Jonathan Dow (PC Barry Stringer) is fitted with a safety harness before being pushed off a scaffold in *"Cry Havoc"*

The gritty, realistic 'look' of *The Bill*'s locations is governed by the Design Department – working in close conjunction with Producers, Directors, Production Managers and Location Managers.

For the exciting episode 'Cry Havoc', which involved Barry Stringer (Jonathan Dow) in pursuit of a dangerous, drug-crazed youth inside a disused power station, the recently gutted Battersea Power Station was used.

The owners of real banks, building societies and Post Offices are understandably reluctant to allow their premises to be used as the scene of any stories relating to armed raids or burglaries – and so these locations have to be created inside normal shop or office sites by the Design Department.

The Location Managers – a minumum of eight work on *The Bill* – not only supervise the finding of locations, they also acquire the necessary permissions and arrange transport of cast, crew and equipment to and from the site, in conjunction with the Production Manager and First Assistant. Ideally, all locations should be within thirty minutes drive of base – travelling further afield eats into valuable shooting time.

Once a location has gone through the design process, it becomes the responsibility of the Property Department to turn the design into reality. Co-ordinating this vital exercise for each operating Unit is Property Master, Dave Hodges. "We are a crew of nine Scenic Operatives – and we do the donkey work," he explained. "We 'dress' each scene with props before recording, deal with any problems during the shoot and 'strike' the scene when recording is finished. It's a matter of logistics, of completing the job in the time allocated. As long as a place looks 'real' on screen then we're happy."

Many props are hired from specialist suppliers. Others have been collected by the Property Department throughout the run of the series. Many thousands of these items are kept in the large, galleried Property Store, a cross between a pawnshop, a jumble sale and a warehouse. Some are true 'props', in the theatrical sense, such as false pillar boxes, bus stop signs and parking meters etc. But in general, items in the store are the real thing.

Drinks on screen are concocted by mixing a burnt sugar (caramel) solution with water. The degree of dilution determines the colour and density of the liquid, ranging from the darkest Port, through Sherry, brandy, whisky and beer, to white wine, gin and vodka.

In September 1989 Colin Tarrant got a message from his agent, telling him to wait by his phone and expect a call from *The Bill* who were urgently trying to fill the role of a new police officer. The call duly came through and Colin was invited to Barlby Road for an interview.

"I went along looking as much like an off-duty policeman as I could - blazer, grey trousers, collar and tie,"

Colin Tarrant

says Colin. "We had a long chat about the character - Mr Monroe - who was to be a stern, authoritarian figure who does everything strictly by-the-book."

The interview went reasonably well, but since Colin hadn't been asked to read for the part, he assumed that he hadn't got the job. "In truth, I'd always thought of myself as ideal casting for left-wing art teachers and liberal-minded social workers in plays by Alan Bleasdale, never a policeman," he says "But there's a line in Arthur Miller's play *Two Way Mirror* in which a character says '...I wake up every morning and I'm shaving my father' and that's true of me - my father has a very stern, authoritarian face and so have I."

And as he later learned, it was that stern look that helped to win him the Monroe role in *The Bill*. "I was called back to Barlby Road next morning, measured for a uniform and told 'You start work on Monday'. One of the producers said he knew I'd look exactly right in a police uniform - and it came as a great shock to me to see that he was right."

Colin was born in Shirebrook, Derbyshire on 14 June 1952, the youngest of three brothers. His parents ran the village grocery shop. A bright boy, he went to grammar school and was a promising footballer who would later have trials for Huddersfield Town. "There wasn't a lot to do in Shirebrook, but there was a Youth Club in the village and one day this huge actor - at least he looked huge to me - turned up there with a bunch of hairdressers and coalminers and they proceeded to perform extracts from plays. To see people acting in the coffee bar of my local youth club, came as a great revelation and got me interested in drama."

The 'huge' actor was Peter Ellis, who at the time ran the Stainsby Arts Centre in the grounds of nearby Hardwick Hall. "I contacted him afterwards and he sent me a copy of Pinter's *The Dumb Waiter*, and although I was far too young at the time, I learned the part of Ben off by heart and from then on I was definitely hooked on the theatre."

Between 1971 and 1974 Colin read English and Drama at Exeter University. This was followed by a year's Post Graduate course in Education at Clifton College, Nottingham.

Much of his early theatre work alternated with spells as a supply teacher. He worked with the Medium Fair Community Theatre in Exeter, and then joined a national tour with the Foco Novo company in 1976-77. Two years of repertory work followed, in Stoke-on-Trent and Nottingham. 1979 and 1980 saw him on national and international tours with the Shared Experience company and the Northern Studio Theatre.

In 1981 he became a member of the first Royal Shakespeare Company to be housed at the Barbican Theatre in London. "I spent two years there playing small to medium-range roles in *The Winter's Tale*, *Titus Andronicus*, *The Two Gentlemen of Verona*, *Money*, *Henry IV Parts I and II*, *Peter Pan* and *Night Shift*. Peter Ellis and Seeta Indrani were also there.

"That was followed by long bouts of unemployment in which I supplemented my acting income by again working as a supply teacher, in the East End of London. The kids gave me a lot of stick because I was an actor. I got a lot of 'How come you're teaching us if you're supposed to be an actor? You can't be much good, sir!' and 'Why aren't you in Coronation Street, sir?'"

Colin's big television break came in

1988 when he played Will Brangwen in the BBC production of DH Lawrence's *The Rainbow*, but when the shooting was finished he went back to teaching. "That really was a freaky experience for the kids - and for me. They'd seen me on Sunday night playing Imogen Stubbs' father in *The Rainbow* and next day I was back in class."

It was soon after the showing of *The Rainbow* that Colin Tarrant's name came up in *The Bill*'s search for Andrew Monroe.

"He started off as the new-broom-sweeping-clean, and the broom had very tough bristles. He had many a run-in with the likes of Burnside," said Colin. "All of that helped to establish the basis of the new Inspector. A line once delivered by Larry Dann, as Alec Peters, sums him up perfectly. He said: 'You don't point Mr Monroe at someone, unless you intend to fire him'."

In time *The Bill*'s scriptwriters began to develop other aspects of the character and we discovered that Monroe does have a heart after all. He's a dedicated family man, the 'world's greatest dad', and he possesses a dry sense of humour. "That's what's so exciting about playing a regular character in a show like *The Bill*," says Colin. "In front of millions of viewers you get the chance to explore and develop different facets of the personality you are portraying. That's always interesting from an actor's point of view."

And thanks to Andrew Monroe's place in the middle ground of the Sun Hill hierarchy, he gets involved in many fascinating storylines. "All paths lead to the Inspector's door," says Colin, "and I get to carpet people too. That's great fun."

And of course, Colin is now reunited once more with Peter Ellis, the actor who originally set him on the road to Sun Hill. "Peter will hate me saying this, but he really is a kind of mentor to me. I'll always be grateful to him for turning up in my village all those years ago."

Larry Dann

Larry Dann made his first film appearance in *Adam and Evelyn* which starred Stewart Granger and Jean Simmons. That was in 1946, when the future Sergeant Alec Peters was just five years old. "The sister of a friend of my father's ran a theatrical agency for children," Larry recalls. "And I originally went along to Denham Studios because it sounded like fun."

Being an inquisitive lad, Larry wandered off during a break in filming. "I went around the back of the set and saw Jean Simmons and Stewart Granger in a passionate clinch. This was before they were married, she must have been only about seventeen at the time. The image has always stuck in my mind and reminds me of my first day in the business."

Little Larry had caught the acting bug at a very early age. He made many more film appearances as a child extra and at the age of eleven told his parents that he definitely wanted to become an actor. "They agreed that I could go to the Corona Academy in Hammersmith, which was about three miles from our home."

The early 1950s was an exciting time for Corona pupils. The British film industry was still in a healthy state in those days and the stagestruck kids were constantly being whisked away to the studios at Pinewood, Denham, Elstree or Twickenham. "I always got lots of work in those days, mainly as an extra," says Larry. "And over the years

I've been in over a hundred films."

His list of theatrical credits is almost as long. In the 1960s he joined Joan Littlewood's renowned Theatre Workshop and was in the original cast of *Oh! What A Lovely War*, at the Theatre Royal, Stratford East. "I learned so much from Joan, and as far as I'm concerned she's one of the most important figures in the British theatre," he says .

Among Larry's film work were appearances in four *Carry On* films, those sometimes delightful, always vulgar, exercises in innuendo and lowest-common-denominator humour. "My first was *Carry On Teacher*, one of the earliest in the series. My last was *Carry On Emmanuel*, in 1978, in which I'd taken over the Jim Dale-type role. It was a disaster and turned out to be the last in the series. Unfortunately, my name was above the title. These days, if I'm involved in an amusing scene in *The Bill*, it's invariably dubbed 'Carry On Up The Bill'. We give out little policemen-shaped statues at our Christmas party - the 'Sierra Oscars'. There's one for 'The Most OTT Performance in a Police Series' another for 'The Nicest Haircut in a Police Series' and so on - I got mine for the 'Best Comedy Performance in a Police Series'.

Back in 1959, the eighteen-year-old Larry Dann was sent to the Granada Television Studios in Manchester to appear in camera tests for *Florizel Street*. "It was to be a six episode serial, possibly thirteen," he remembers. "I played a character called Dennis Tanner and acted with a lady called Pat Phoenix who played his mother.

Of course, *Florizel Street* became Coronation Street, the longest running TV saga of them all but the part of Dennis Tanner eventually went to another young actor, Philip Lowrie.

Larry is very ambitious. He is positively looking forward to playing other roles in the future, to stretch his talent and to do more directing in the theatre (in March '91 he directed the Ben Travers farce *Cuckoo in the Nest* at the Shaw Festival Theatre in Ontario). "That's where I differ from Alec Peters - I'm keen, full of energy, and eager to do more work; he lost all his ambition when they changed the rules of policing.

"Alec is an old-fashioned copper in the '*Dixon of Dock Green*' mould - when they used to clip the ear of any youngsters caught misbehaving. But now that the rule book has taken over, it's not really him anymore. He'll carry on until 'til he gets his pension, then he'll retire to his allotment. I most certainly won't be doing that."

Larry lives with his wife Liz, a costume designer, in a delightful Edwardian house in a village setting to the west of London. Unfortunately their marriage has been touched with sadness. "We've never been able to have children," says Larry. "Like one-in-six couples we are infertile. We've tried twice to have a test-tube baby. It was a painful process for Liz and we decided not to try again. Now I'm too old to adopt a child. Life is cruel sometimes."

Larry divides his spare time between walking his dog Gimli, listening to jazz, writing television scripts with his good friend Roger Leach (who played Tom Penny in *The Bill*) and indulging his passion for golf and cricket (he's a founder member of Chadwick, an actors' and musicians' XI).

But he definitely won't go anywhere near an allotment.

Andrew Paul is an East End boy, born in Mile End on 17 March 1961, one of five brothers. The family later moved just a few miles up the road, to Stoke Newington where Andrew went to school. He caught the acting bug early.

Andrew Paul

"I must have been about three when I first saw on TV an old black-and-white film of the brilliant Fred Astaire, that got me started," he remembers. "I was always dancing - a real little show off. And for as long as I can remember I wanted to be in the entertainment business."

And Andrew has never been afraid to put himself in the frame as an actor - even when he wasn't exactly suited to a role. He explains: "When I was a kid, a film producer turned up at our school - he was looking for a small blond boy to play a part in a Children's Film Foundation production. Now by no stretch of the imagination was I blond, but I was so determined to become an actor that I begged the teacher to let the producer see me."

Impressed by the boy's obvious determination, the producer did interview Andrew, and his parents, twice. He didn't win a role in the movie, but he was recommended to the Anna Scher Children's Theatre.

At fourteen he played his first professional role, as one of the boys who demolish an old man's house in Graham Greene's celebrated short story 'The Destructors' which was part of the *Shades of Greene* series produced by Thames in 1975.

Other strong parts followed for Andrew, including those of Frank Ross's (Tom Bell) son Paul in *Out*, in 1978, and Betts in *Scum*, Alan Clarke's film version of Roy Minton's uncompromising study of borstal life, in 1979. "I worked quite a lot between the ages of fourteen and nineteen," he recalls. "But after that I had long spells without getting much - that's just the way it goes in this business."

In the summer of 1989 Andrew worked on *The Bill* in a small part as a Special Constable, and in his usual forthright manner asked the producer, Michael Ferguson, if there was a chance of a regular part in the series. "As it happened they were looking for someone, to play PC Quinnan. I was interviewed by the producers and subsequently given the part - and I had to start almost immediately."

There are a number of similarities between Andrew Paul and Dave Quinnan. They are both Londoners, they both come from large families, both come from working-class backgrounds and both are avid football fans (Andrew supports Arsenal).

"But that's where the likeness ends, says Andrew. "For a start, Quinnan is single and always chasing women, whereas I'm happily married, to Laura, who I first met when I was eighteen and she was fifteen. We have a lovely son, Ben, and are currently expecting our second child. Dave Quinnan is far too selfish to be a husband and a caring father - I certainly can't imagine him changing nappies."

Nevertheless, different though they might be, Andrew is quick to defend Quinnan's reputation as a police officer. "Some people thought he was a nasty piece of work when he first arrived at Sun Hill but since then we've developed other aspects of his character and made him less two dimensional.

"Okay, he's a bit of a wide-boy, he's a wind-up merchant and he's definitely naive when it comes to the gentle things in life. But he's also very sharp and a good copper who thinks on his toes. He gets results in an unconventional way which isn't always by the book."

One episode which displayed Quinnan's intuitive, quick-witted method of policing was 'What Kind of Man', written by Christopher Russell and directed by Chris Lovett. "Quinnan went to a primary school where a break-in had been reported. A charity worker was giving a talk to the kids all about 'Dogs in Danger', and he was accompanied by a mascot, a big toy dog dressed in red. Something instantly clicked in Quinnan's mind. He rushed back to Sun Hill and looked up the witness statements on a couple of child murder cases. In one of them a drunk had reported seeing a 'big dog in a red coat driving a car'. The information eventually led to the arrest of the bogus charity worker. Brownlow recommended Dave for a commendation for that one - for 'meritorious alertness and use of initiative'. I was proud of him that day."

Despite being one of Britain's most versatile actresses, Carolyn Pickles was surprised when she was asked to take on the DCI role in *The Bill*. "Initially, I suspected that Michael Chapman chose me because of my family connections with the Law. Or maybe he just saw me as an authoritarian figure, which I'm not at all."

And, like all newcomers to *The Bill*, Carolyn stepped into P amount of trepidation. "It's always difficult to join an established and successful cast," she says. "And to act as if I was 'in charge' made it even more difficult. I had quite

Carolyn Pickles

a hard time to begin with, but I handled it by sticking my jaw out and drawing on my in-built northern tenacity."

In preparation for the role of Kim Reid, Carolyn got to know a real female DCI, based at a West London police station. "She's one of the lads, a very bright girl who is as quick and sharp-witted as any of the men around her. I doubt if any female could do a DCI's job successfully without that element of humour. It's probably the best way to deal with all those maverick male egos."

Kim Reid made a classy entrance at Sun Hill - with a sandwich in one hand

and a prisoner arm-locked in the other. "And she's never looked back," says Carolyn. "She'll go a long way in the force, and she is well aware that her performance at Sun Hill is being carefully monitored by those who can advance her career."

Carolyn's own career has been equally successful. Born in Halifax, she is the second child and only daughter of the sometimes controversial Judge James Pickles. "I used to watch my father when he was a barrister, a job which definitely has an air of theatricality about it. He was a fine actor, a master of timing. Later, when he became a recorder, then a Judge, he would often discuss cases with my brothers and I. It was fascinating and there was a time when I seriously considered the Law as a career."

It was, perhaps, the distant influence of other relatives which steered Carolyn towards the acting profession. Her aunt, Christina Pickles, is an actress and the celebrated radio star and character actor Wilfred Pickles was her great uncle. "I see the advantages of having within one's experience people who have succeeded in the business. It gives one con-

fidence and shows that it is possible to have a career on the stage or screen."

Carolyn read drama at Manchester University, intending to pursue an acting career, while keeping open the option of teaching if things didn't work out. One of her earliest TV roles came in 1975 when she played "...a tart who was picked-up by Eddie Yates in *Coronation Street*. I ruined Deirdrie and Ray's new coffee table by leaving a burning cigarette on it!"

She made her film debut in *Agatha*, with Vanessa Redgrave and Dustin Hoffman in 1978 but her big break came in the following year when she appeared as Marion in *Tess*. Perhaps her best-remembered TV roles prior to *The Bill* were the lead in *Bluebell*, the life story of the famous Folies Bergere dancer, and the part of Sally Bilton in LWT's wartime drama *We'll Meet Again*.

Then came marriage to Tark (short for Tarquin), an artist and designer who has written and illustrated a number of children's books. The couple now have two daughters, Lucy and Hettie, to complement Tark's two sons Tod and Theo, from his previous marriage. "For a long time I felt I was going into interviews reeking of motherhood. Once, soon after beginning on *The Bill*, I slipped up and said 'disposable' instead of 'disposal' - I must have had nappies on the brain."

Carolyn has recently displayed her talent for comedy, as the prissy Simone in the BBC's *May To December*, with Anton Rodgers. But it's obviously DCI Kim Reid who takes up most of her time these days.

And among her most avid fans is her recently retired father. "He has always followed my career with great interest and when I first got the part of Kim Reid he sent me a job description and a list of qualities that the police look for in a potential DCI. He's a great fan of *The Bill* and he wanted me to be as convincing as possible."

"I no longer have analytical thoughts about Ted Roach," says Tony Scannell. "He's taken over a huge part of my life. Half the time I don't know whether he's me, or I'm him."

Tony Scannell was born in Kinsale, County Cork, on 14 August 1945. His father, Tommy Scannell, played professional football, and won two international caps for The Republic of Ireland between 1954

Tony Scannell

and 1956. When he signed for Third Division Southend United in 1949, young Tony stayed with relatives in Kinsale while the family moved to England.

Tony eventually completed an apprenticeship as a toolmaker and then rejoined the family at their home in Folkestone, Kent. "I did various jobs on the seafront there, from deck-chair attendant to singing bingo caller. I was also a TV salesman and worked for *Miss London*, the recruitment magazine."

In 1966 Tony joined the RAF as a photographic interpreter and stayed for five years. He was posted to Cyprus where, in his spare time, he became a radio DJ with his own late-night easy listening hour on British Forces radio.

"I suppose I first fell in love with the theatre when I got back to England, and began putting on shows of my own on the base," he says.

By the time he left the RAF in 1970, Tony had decided to pursue a theatrical career and began by getting a job as an Assistant Stage Manager at the Cambridge Arts' Theatre. "Although I was

twenty-seven by the time I got my Equity card, I decided I ought to go to a drama school to find out what acting was really all about. I got into the E15 acting school, in Loughton Essex, and thoroughly enjoyed my time there."

His thesis play at E15 was Noel Coward's *Private Lives* which was directed by Jack Watling. Watling was impressed by Tony's performance as Elyot Chase, and he invited him to join his company at the Frinton Repertory Theatre. "We did seven plays in seven weeks, I remember. It was a great learning process for me."

Tony later joined Joan Littlewood's Theatre Workshop. "I never actually worked with the legendary lady, but she was always around, running things. I stayed a year and a half."

Later still, he played Winston Churchill and Max Miller, among other wartime figures, in the touring version of the WWII musical *Happy as a Sandbag*. He acted at the King's Head pub/theatre in Islington, then joined the Hull Truck Company and for a year was a member of the National Theatre, appearing in *Four Weeks in the City* and Sean O'Casey's *The Plough and the Stars*. "That was the first time I'd played an Irishman. I'd mostly been given American parts up till then, because my accent lends itself very well to that way of speaking."

Tony's first television role was a small part in *Little Lord Fauntleroy*. Other parts followed in *Armchair Thriller*, *The Professionals* - and as an Irish-American terrorist in the Victorian detective series *Cribb*.

'Although Tony has never regretted giving up the RAF life for an actor's life - "the money wasn't as good in acting, but I'd have done it for nothing" - he had, nevertheless, left the profession and was working with a marine salvage company in Moville, Northern Ireland when his agent told him that his name had cropped up in the search for detectives on *The Bill*.

"It seems that the casting director Pat O'Connell had remembered seeing me at the King's Head in *The New Garbo*, and thought of me for Roach. I came over as quickly as possible and I got the job."

Originally the character was only to be included in the second and third episodes of the first series. But the part grew and Ted Roach became one of Sun Hill's permanent fixtures.

It's hard to imagine the slow-eyed, quick-tempered Ted Roach with any accent other than Tony's soft Irish lilt - yet the character was planned as a cockney. "We soon changed that," says Tony. "And the fact that we could do that underlines one of the great strengths of *The Bill* - realism is paramount so the role, once cast, was adapted to my characteristics."

Like almost everyone else in the cast, Tony enjoys the spontaneous method of recording *The Bill*. "The results speak for themselves; we know that many people in the business - people who don't normally watch much telly when they're off duty - actually make a point of tuning into *The Bill*. That's very gratifying."

Nowadays, Ted Roach alias Tony Scannell, gets more than his fair share of attention from *The Bill*'s female fans. "I'd be lying if I said I didn't enjoy all that," says Tony. "I think it's basically because, for all his bravado, Roach is lacking in confidence - and he needs a bit of looking after. There's no badness in him either, he's a good person at heart. He just falls foul of people sometimes and finds it very difficult to bite the bullet when he knows darn well he should. He's a loser

in that respect."

Tony divides his spare time between playing golf - a handicap of thirteen - and working on the renovation of his house, a three-bedroom terraced house in south east London. He bought the property late in 1990 and has been working on it ever since. "The previous owners had been very fond of dark brown paint and vinyl. I wanted to create a feeling of light and space, so I started knocking down walls...at least I think it was me - it may have been Ted."

Nick Stringer found he had to make a great personal sacrifice for the role of Sun Hill's Collator, Ron Smollett. "Ever since I was eighteen I'd worn a moustache," explains Nick. "But when I came for my interview there was great consternation over whether I'd be prepared to shave it off or not. And, of course, all my professional photographs showed me with the moustache. So, out came the Tippex to remove it from the pictures and see how I'd look without it."

Nick Stringer

Naturally Nick was prepared to wield the razor in the cause of his art and he duly became PC Ron Smollett, Sun Hill's third Collator after Reg Hollis and Cathy Marshall.

"Ron is very much his own man," says Nick. "He's been around a long time - twenty years in the Traffic Division - and knows how to put his hands on anything from a quick respray on a scratched Panda to tickets for the opera. He also has a healthy disrespect for Sergeants and Inspectors.

"Really, he's a law unto himself with his own way of doing things. But for all that, he is a very good Collator. He's like a walking computer, he's got it all up there in his brain. If, for instance, there's a sudden spate of handbag snatching on the Sun Hill manor, Ron will quickly recall to mind all the local 'handbag snatchers' of old and he'll have their files out in a flash. He has the memory of an elephant."

Nick was born in Torquay in August 1948, but spent most of his childhood in Bristol, before his family eventually returned to their roots in Birmingham when he was 12. As a young man it seemed that he was destined for a nine-to-five career when he joined Lloyds Bank as a trainee manager. "But there was always a doubt in my mind," he says. "I was constantly nagged by something the interviewer had told me when I first applied for the job - 'Young man,' he said, 'you could be an Assistant Manager by the time you're forty.' I was only nineteen at the time."

Nick had long harboured an ambition to work in the theatre and he now took the plunge by leaving the security of the bank, to work behind the scenes in Birmingham's Hippodrome and Alexandra Theatres. "I wanted to see what the life was like. I worked on variety shows and loved every minute of it. And I decided to go to drama school."

He moved to London in 1970 and enrolled at the Guildhall School of Music and Drama, which at that time was situated near Fleet Street. "We had a great time, sharing the pubs at lunchtimes with the printers and the journalists," Nick remembers.

"I left Guildhall in 1973 and was very lucky to go straight to the Liverpool Everyman to work alongside people like Anthony Sher, Jonathan Pryce, Bernard Hill and Julie Walters. I stayed with the Everyman for two years, during which time we produced the Beatles' story, *John, Paul, George, Ringo and Bert*. I played twelve parts in the show, including Adolf Hitler, Allan Klein and an aircraft landing at JFK Airport."

Nick continued to work in repertory companies up and down the country and he played occasional roles on television. "I was Frank Harvey, the relief manager of the Rovers Return in *Coronation Street*," he recalls. "That was around the time when Fred Feast, who played Fred Gee, left the *Street* in a cloud of controversy. I alternated the job with David Daker who is now well-known for his role in *Boon*. And I appeared in lots of series *Minder*, *Shoestring*, *The Professionals*, *Dempsey and Makepeace*, *Auf Wiedersehen Pet* and *Only Fools and Horses* to name but

a few. I was even a rather nasty character, called Terry Mitchell who ran a Fagin-like stolen goods racket in 'Homebeat', an early hour-long episode of *The Bill* written by Christopher Russell."

Nick has also appeared in a handful of excellent films including *Clockwise*, in which he played a detective on the trail of John Cleese, *Personal Services* - as an inept policeman, and most memorably *The Long Good Friday* in which he played one of the gangsters hung upside-down on meat-hooks in an abbatoir, by Bob Hoskins. "That was an absolutely horrendous day," Nick remembers. "We were left dangling there while they prepared the set-ups and so on. It was so uncomfortable and it was impossible to talk to the chap hanging beside me. Every so often one of us would pass out. When we came round again there was an over-enthusiastic St John's Ambulanceman asking for a graphic description of the moments before losing conciousness. Bob Hoskins was very concerned about us, and at one point he took my weight on his back to stop me from passing out again."

It took Nick several days to recover from the ordeal. But the resulting image was one of the most powerful and disturbing in the history of British cinema. "Now that really was a case of suffering for one's art. It makes shaving off my moustache seem like child's play - mind you, I still miss it. But I doubt if Ron Smollett will allow me to re-cultivate it for a while."

'I've led a charmed life as an actor," says Graham Cole. Which is quite surprising when you consider that he actually refused to go on stage in what was to be his debut performance.

"It was a school play in Harlow, in which my character was supposed to have water poured over him," says Graham. "I had to sit in a bath with my legs dangling over the sides. But some lads came into a rehearsal

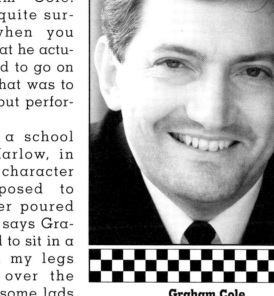

Graham Cole

and took the Mickey out of my Michelinman physique, and that was it - I walked off the stage and refused to return."

Graham was born in Willesden, north London, on 16 March 1952. When he was four the family moved to Harlow in Essex. "Much of my youth was spent working with animals - I was an RSPCA Junior Leader at a Pets' Corner in Harlow. Kids used to come out from London to see the cows, horses and ducks. And I'm glad to report that the place is still going strong."

Both Graham's parents were St John's Ambulance volunteers and he worked alongside them for seven years. "Apart from animals, First Aid was my only other love. So, when it came to choosing a career, it all boiled down to working with animals or people."

People won - and he became a hospital porter at the Herts & Essex Hospital in Bishop's Stortford. At eighteen, having worked his way through various depart-

ments, he transferred to the Harlow Hospital and trained as an orthopaedic technician, under the Royal National Orthopaedic Hospital scheme. "I slapped plaster around broken arms and legs and assisted the surgeons during reduction and traction operations. I did it for four years. Then I came home one day and decided I was going to work in show-business."

So, in the summer of 1973 Graham Cole took his first tentative steps towards stardom by becoming a Redcoat at a holiday camp in Camber Sands. There he met his future wife, Cherry: she was sixteen at the time and had just won the camp's beauty contest. He later worked at other holiday camps, all the while writing off for every suitable job advertised in *The Stage*. "I finally landed a job which lasted for two-and-a-half years, with a group called The Bel Canto Singers. We did backing work for various singers in panto and summer seasons in the mid-'70s."

Throughout the remainder of the seventies and into the eighties Graham continued to work steadily, alternating between variety, rep and TV. "The television work came in between seasons. For instance, I'd go in for a day and appear in a sketch on the *Kenny Everett Show*, and I later played various monsters in *Dr Who* - I was never a Dalek though, I was too big for that."

One day Graham was called into *The Bill* studios to do a walk-on part in a drugs-raid scene. "It just grew from there.When the show went to its half-hour format I was asked to come in for a couple of 'dummy run' episodes which were primarily to test the equipment and were never to be broadcast. After that I was called back to appear in 'Light Duties'."

Graham learned that he'd been made a regular member of the cast when he attended the press launch of the half-hour format. "They were handing out cards showing pictures of the cast - and there was my face above the name 'PC Tony Stamp'."

The role of Tony Stamp evolved slowly, but surely, into one of The Bill's most popular and enduring characters. Real policemen, in particular admire Graham's performance and on one occasion when the actor was out shopping with his wife, a uniformed constable crossed the street to shake his hand.

"Tony is an eighteen year man, which means he's probably one of the most experienced policemen at Sun Hill," says Graham. "But he doesn't want promotion, because of all the paperwork. He's quite happy being a 'spearhead', sitting in his car, listening to the crackle of a message on the radio and then racing off to deal with the situation - providing it isn't 'domestic' stuff which he really can't handle. Of course, he can be a bit over-conscientious at times and often puts his foot in it, right up to his neck."

The consistency of his performance as Stamp, stems from Graham's insistence on doing thorough and regular research, particularly concerning Tony's driving of the Area Car. "I've been on the Hendon driving course three times. And I go out with the real Area Cars at least twice a year, purely for research purposes, and I'm still fascinated with those guys and the way they do their job."

Another aspect of Stamp's character is his expertise in martial arts. One episode called for him to teach a women's group the rudiments of self-defence. In the interest of accuracy Graham again went to Hendon to work out with the P T Instructors.

Graham has something of a daredevil reputation around the Sun Hill headquarters, as he always insists on doing his own driving stunts. "I've only been refused twice," he recalls. "When a stunt man had to fly over the bonnet, and during the second part of a crash which was deemed just a bit too dangerous for me." In 'Married to the Job', written by Roger Leach, Stamp's proposal of marriage was refused by his long-time girlfriend, Julie. This rather pleased Graham. "Women frighten the life out of him, which is probably why he's remained single for so long. The producers once asked me if I'd mind if Stamp was married with two children. But that's my situation in reality - Cherry and I have two lovely kids, Matthew and Laura - and I felt decidedly uneasy about art imitating life quite so closely. I pleaded with them not to do it and to let Tony remain the eternal bachelor."

Rewind: to one of Jonathan ("call me Jo") Dow's earliest TV roles, as a young GP in an episode of *London's Burning*. The storyline concerned a window cleaner who had fallen off his ladder and was impaled on the iron railings fence of the surgery. The young doctor rushed out to administer drugs and comfort until the fire brigade arrived to attempt - unsuccessfully - to save the man's life.

"I heard later that the poor guy playing the window cleaner suffered from vertigo," recalls Jo. "But he hadn't told anyone because he'd wanted the part so desperately. He must have gone through agonies because he spent half the day clinging to the ladder while the crew set the scene below, while we rehearsed, and of course while we recorded our scenes. Through it all he was as white as a sheet."

Fast forward: several months have passed and Jo Dow has become a Sun Hill regular, pounding the beat as Midland-born PC Barry Stringer. "Now I receive a *Bill* script called 'Cry Havoc' in which I have to fall off a ledge a hundred feet up inside a disused power station. The script was written by Russell Lewis, the very same actor who I'd last seen quaking up that ladder. I thought there was a certain irony there."

Russell Lewis's 'Cry Havoc', directed by Stuart Urban, proved one of *The Bill*'s most exciting episodes to date. A drug-crazed youth, Gary Mabbs, stabbed Alec Peters as the Sergeant attempted to

Jonathan Dow

apprehend him. Meanwhile, Stringer was driving back to Sun Hill to replace his radio which had gone on the blink. Mabbs, on the run, was hit by Stringer's car but he ran on. Seeing blood on the windscreen, Stringer thought he had injured the youth, and because of the broken radio was oblivious of the stabbing incident. Feeling guilty about the accident, he gave chase on foot and followed Mabbs into the power station - losing his hat in the process.

Eventually the chase took the two men high into the rafters of the building. A fight ensued 150 feet above the ground, with Stringer using his broken radio as a flail. To make matters worse, an angry rottweiller guard dog was on the prowl below. Mabbs refused to give himself up and escaped again. Stringer caught up with him on a ledge but Mabbs shoved him over the edge and the terrified PC saved himself only by grabbing at some overhanging netting and hanging on for dear life. The rottweiller attacked Mabbs as he attempted to dislodge Stringer by hitting him with a lump of wood. The youth lost his balance and fell to his doom.

Meanwhile, the Sun Hill squad had mounted a search for Stringer and his whereabouts were revealed when Tony Stamp spotted some children playing with his hat near the power station.

Jo Dow dubbed the episode 'Die Hard' as it was shot in a very exciting and cinematic style by Stuart Urban. The main action took place inside the old Battersea Power Station, which had been almost completely gutted in readiness for its proposed redevelopment.

Jo insisted on making the stunt fall himself as he felt it was vital for viewers to see the look of genuine fear on Stringer's face. "I wore a harness and and was also attached to a safety rope. The problem was some protruding scaffolding poles, over which I had to leap before I'd feel the pull of the rope. Stuart told me to show some real fear when I went over - which wasn't difficult to do. In fact, the scream I let out was a bit too piercing and we had to dub on a slightly more 'Butch' version afterwards."

Another scene called for the two actors to walk across the iron girder rafters, no more than a foot wide and with a 100 foot drop to the floor below. "The stunt team made it more reassuring by attaching wide wooden planks to the underside of the girders. Going one way was okay, but coming back was seriously scary because the wind inside the building seemed to be a lot stronger. The only shot we couldn't do shows feet shuffling along the girder with a view of the ground and the dog below. It took a very brave stunt man to do that while carrying the camera and pointing it at his feet."

Once these dangerous scenes were in the can, the stunt arranger, Ian Gillard, presented Jo with a highly prized Stunt Association tee-shirt - for services rendered beyond the call of duty.

'Cry Havoc' was also an innovative episode, in that it captured certain inaccessible images via a fibre optic cable linked to a VTR. "The cable was attached to a microphone pole which followed my feet as I slid down a bank during the chase into the power station," says Jo. "The results were astonishing."

Jo was born in Redditch, Worcestershire, on 23 March 1965. The Dow family are of Scottish descent and have a long association with the medical profession.

"My father, grandfather, Godfather, uncles and one of my three brothers are all doctors. My early ambition was to be an artist, but I never got round to doing it, and acting kind of took over."

In 1984, after a prep and public school education in Bromsgrove and Worcester, Jo went to the Guildhall Drama School in London and acted with the National Youth Theatre in the summer months. "I left drama school without completing the course, having got an agent and job - playing the Head Boy in Alan Bennett's Forty Years On in Cardiff. I did theatre for quite a while after that, some rep, some work in London. I was in Nana at the Mermaid, and Les Liaisons Dangereuses. It's a wonderful play, but I only had a small part in it, the waiting around drove me mad."

He made his TV debut as a student in After the War and also appeared as a Spitfire pilot in A Piece of Cake. Then came his brief appearance in London's Burning which was followed by a series as Penelope Keith's secretary Tim, in No Job for a Lady. Then his agent sent him along to The Bill, who were in the process of casting two provincial constables - Loxton and Stringer. "I'd never used my Redditch accent professionally before, but now it came in really handy. They asked me what sort of character I'd like to play, I said someone who's broadminded, not a racist, or sexist copper. I thought it would be interesting to see how such a liberal-minded character is affected by the job."

Here, Jo was reminded of another touch of irony. "During the run of Les Liaisons I'd talked with another actor about what we'd like to do in the future. He said he'd love a long-running part in The Bill. I said I'd never do that - I wouldn't like the uniform..."

Colin Alldridge originally auditioned for the Dave Quinnan role in *The Bill*. "But they thought I looked too young for Quinnan, and of course the part eventually went to Andrew Paul," says Colin. "Naturally I was disappointed - *The Bill* was one of the few TV series that had really impressed me. Soon afterwards I got a call from my agent saying that *The Bill* had decided to create a part for me."

Colin Alldridge

The role was that of Phil Young, Sun Hill's youngest constable, somewhat green around the gills. "That was in October 1989 and I was sent to do some research with real policemen in Kilburn," recalls Colin. "I went out with a squad car as they went to sort out pub brawls and that sort of thing. It was all fascinating stuff."

But then, in the early hours of a Saturday morning, the young actor found himself involved in a high speed chase in pursuit of an allegedly stolen car. "The car crashed into another vehicle, and the occupants ran off. My driver and his mate got out to give chase and I followed. One of the youths went over a wall and then doubled-back, which meant he was running towards me. Without thinking I just dived out of the shadows and rugby tackled him."

The youth immediately gave himself up and was arrested by the real police. "The worst part about it was that I'd landed in a pile of dog crap. It rather took the shine off my moment of glory!"

Colin Alldridge was born in Bournemouth, on 19 June 1965, although his father's work in the motor trade took the family to Chester when Colin was still a small child. "I hated school," he remembers. "I never really felt comfortable and was often bullied because I was so small. I used to fantasise about escaping to America and becoming a cop there, like Starsky and Hutch."

At sixteen Colin played a small part in a community theatre production of *Toad of Toad Hall*. "And I knew I wanted more – I'd got the bug. I enrolled on a three week drama course but almost didn't go, because my father had been made redundant and we were going back to Bournemouth to live. But someone persuaded me to go and catch up with the family afterwards."

Colin then took a Drama Foundation course at the Poole College of Further Education, before signing for a three year course at the Drama Centre, in Chalk Farm, north London . "That was an intense, highly concentrated period of learning and discovery. It snapped me out of my shyness."

At twenty-one, Colin fulfilled his childhood ambition by travelling for six months in the USA "America was everything I'd imagined it would be. I met lots of people, went out with lots of girls, had lots of fun sunbathing and water-skiing. It was one of the best times of my life."

Colin returned to England on the day his visa expired. Then, in order to qualify for his Equity card, he joined another would-be actor, Rob Faulkener, in a cabaret act which they performed in various pubs in Bournemouth.

After a second spell in America, Colin returned once more to England and won a part in a play called *Wild at Heart*. "It turned out to be the biggest load of old tat imaginable - nothing to do with the David Lynch film. To remedy this the director decided to turn it into a musical, and because I was one of the few people in the show who could sing and dance I had a big song and dance number at the finale. What had begun as a very poor piece of theatre, turned out to be a great showcase for me, and by the end of the run I had found myself an agent."

But it was to be another seven months before Colin won his second professional role, as Steve the Sensible Driver, in an educational video. "Then, in another video which graphically described to young soldiers the dangers of unprotected sex, I played a squaddie who had contracted AIDS."

More work followed in TV commercials and pop videos before being brought in for questioning at Sun Hill.

If Colin numbers his entry at Sun Hill among his more memorable moments, then his exit from the programme was to be equally dramatic. Phil Young had never fitted comfortably into the Sun Hill set-up. An over-sensitive soul, he was unable to cultivate that peculiar professional sense of humour which sees most policemen through the horrors of the job. Consequently the stresses of policing led him to a tragic end.

"Without doubt the most exciting episodes for me were the last ones I did, in which Phil starts to crack up. "Things had begun to go wrong for him several months earlier when he'd discovered the body of a fifteen-year-old girl who had committed suicide. Towards the end he latched on to Norika Datta. But when she refused to go out with him he attacked her. After that it was was very clear that he had lost it and when he found another suicide he cracked up completely and took his own life by feeding exhaust fumes into his car."

Colin Alldridge is now pursuing his musical career, but he'll never forget the time he walked the Sun Hill beat.

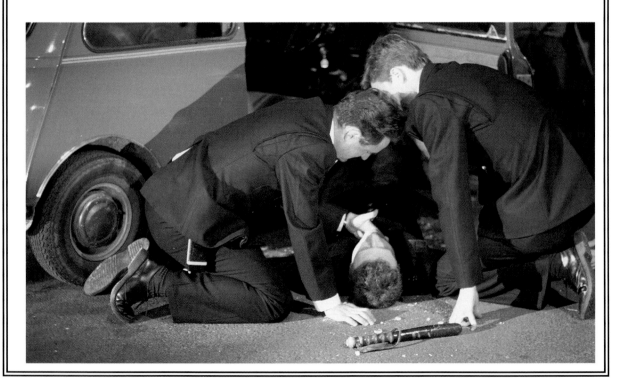

The Story So Far...
1984–1991

1984

October

* PCs Carver and Edwards arrest a suspected car thief, but he's a police informant whose help is needed on the streets, and is released to assist with a 'bust'.
* An attempted child abduction is reported but the suspect slashes his wrists before police can question him.
* A civilian makes a citizen's arrest when a pickpocket dips into his jacket only to discover that the man had sewn fish- hooks into the lining.

November

* The Sun Hill squad are severely reprimanded when a young girl's quest for the bright lights ends in disaster.
* A military style operation is mounted to deal with heroin abuse on a nearby estate.
* PC Litten, investigating the theft of a necklace, is set up by an informant who claims to know the burglars, but is in fact after the insurance reward.

December

* DI Galloway reprimands Litten for not asking for positive ID when a man collects a car from the pound who is not the rightful owner.

1985

January

* Mullins, a safe cracksman who has 'temporarily' escaped from prison, reluctantly helps three thugs who have removed a safe from a factory. A fight ensues and he is killed. Edwards later arrests the men.
* Ackland and Carver uncover a counterfeit perfume factory in the docklands area.
* Galloway attempts to nail Cohen, a distributor of pornography.

END SERIES ONE

November

* PC Lyttleton arrives at Sun Hill.
* A power cut causes havoc at the station when they find that their radios have not been charged.
* When an 8 year-old girl goes missing, a search is mounted, whilst officers check on known sex-offenders. She is found happily making cakes with a widow.
* A cigarette factory worker who has been "pregnant" for thirteen months is discovered smuggling cigarettes out in her "baby bulge".

December

* Racial trouble flares on the Dairy Street Estate and a Neighbourhood Watch meeting is disrupted by Leftist agitators.
* Cryer, Roach and others prepare for their annual sea fishing trip to Margate, but it is cancelled as an armed robbery is reported at a betting shop.
* PC Frank is shot by the robber who takes a woman hostage in a block of flats. Cryer negotiates and is about to disarm him when Galloway and detectives burst in and shoot the robber.
* Edwards and Carver return an escaped pig to a city farm.
* Con men are caught delivering a wardrobe to a house. There was a burglar hiding inside the wardrobe.

1986

January

* Sgt. Penny tries to impose a no smoking ban at the station. His wife turns to Cryer for help when she tells him that Penny is beating her up.
* Carver and Muswell have a fight in the lavatory over Muswell's cynical attitude towards an attempted rape.
* A con artist is caught emptying gas meters but the victims won't identify him as he always gives them a good discount.

February

* A 5-a-side football match is organised during Community Fortnight with Sun Hill taking on the local youth club. Martella, who is in goal, takes some flak when they lose 5-2.
* Everyone is told to be at the retirement party for the Chief Super's clerk, which is being held in a room above a pub. Burnside - a detective sergeant from another manor - is there and doesn't seem to be popular with anyone. Some stolen Scotch turns up behind the bar and Roach drives home drunk and crashes into someone's front garden. He is reported to the Super by Hollis, who hopes it will help his application for the vacant clerk's position. Roach is let off the hook when he traps sheepskin coat thieves in a cold store.

END SERIES TWO

1987

September

* A man armed with an iron bar watching Sun Hill is questioned. His brother suffered injuries during the miners' strike and died from a brain haemorrhage, and he knows that PC Muswell hit him.
* Hollis is unbearably smug after single-handedly disarming and handcuffing a man in a Labour Exchange.
* A drugs raid on a community centre leads to fighting in the streets. Petrol bombs are thrown and officers are sent into the fray in riot gear.

October

* DAC Wainwright is to inspect the station, so all are engaged on cleaning operations. Hollis is nominated as Federation rep. and impresses the DAC by talking to him about stress.
* In bad weather, Cryer knocks down and kills an old lady. He is cleared but Insp. Kite is very hostile towards him. Galloway, however, is protective.
* Edwards is getting married so Carver arranges a booze-up at a local pub. At his party Edwards gets drunk and has a row with Smith. They strip Edwards naked and lock him out.
* Roach is stabbed in the backside by louts in a pub.

November

* The roads around Sun Hill are clogged by protesting taxi drivers after Galloway gets a parking ticket, bumps a taxi and arrests the driver. He is later told to drop the case.
* The Yard's Complaints Investigation Bureau arrive following a report that two bent coppers issued a fine on the spot which they pocketed. Shaw loses his temper during questioning and Roach and Carver later bring in the culprits who turn out to be bogus PCs.
* Ackland and Martella arrest a man who is dressed as a bear.
* Martella applies to the Bermuda Police Force but, after being punched during a fight and then failing to prevent a suicide

jumper, she feels she is not up to the job and withdraws the application.

December

* Carver arrests a man for holding up petrol stations in the nude.
* Martella goes home sick after having bought a bar of chocolate possibly poisoned by a supermarket employee.
* Penny is shot in the stomach after investigating a complaint from a landlord about a crazy woman and her cats. He is trapped in the flat out of reach of his radio but is eventually found and taken to hospital.

END SERIES THREE

1988

July

* Sgt. Penny, on light duties as a result of his gunshot wound, insists he is perfectly fit, but he is swigging alcohol and tablets to deaden the pain and develops a drink problem. Later he breaks down and confesses all to Cryer.
* Roach is acting DI after the departure of Galloway. Inspector Christine Frazer arrives at Sun Hill a day early, out of uniform, and Roach, unaware of who she is, tries to chat her up in the pub.
* New PC, Peter Ramsey, arrives in a Porsche. He has a reputation for cheating at cards. Ramsey drives away from a garage without paying but the owner is a friend of Cryer's who orders him to settle up and warns that he will be watching him closely in future.
* Smith and Ackland are shot at by an armed robber. An armed policeman narrowly misses Smith when he returns fire. Smith wallops him.

August

* Roach goes against Conway's orders in arresting a suspect named Duffy, and is accused of deliberate disobedience. Frazer wants to recommend Roach for promotion but Conway says that Brownlow would never make him DI.
* Frazer's old friend, Burnside, is made DI. Cryer reports him for slapping a skinhead prisoner around the face and describes him as 'bent'. Frazer warns him about 'malicious gossip'. The prisoner had also been head-butted by Roach after spitting at him. He turns out to be an undercover agent, DS Trimlet.
* Roach fails a firearms refresher course and is no longer entitled to carry firearms. Confesses to a barmaid that he has a horror of "blowing somebody away".

September

* Melvin reveals to Edwards that he is a Born Again Christian.
* Penny blows his top working in an overheated CAD Room. The electrician, mending the thermostat, irritates him with constant chatter and when Penny spills his coffee, putting the computer out of action, he loses control and attacks the electrician. There is now no question that he should take further convalescence.
* Whilst carrying out home improvements, a man finds a skeleton standing upright behind the plaster wall in his flat.

October

* Ackland and Edwards enter a shed and see rows of battery cages crammed with chickens, some alive, many dead. The owner, Stokes, armed with a shotgun, refuses to let them leave. Peters arrives, but Stokes handcuffs him and Edwards together. Melvin and Stamp are sent to investigate, Stokes fires a shot, Ackland creates a diversion by releasing some hens and between them they manage to disarm the gunman.
* Two black youths are questioned in separate incidents and both give the same name - Winston Kingsley. Brownlow meets a solicitor representing Kingsley who claims he has been stopped and searched thirteen times in the last two weeks. But newly-arrived DC Lines hints that the locals have all been giving the same name when they've been stopped.
* Roach dates Frazer but is advised by Burnside not to expect too much from the first night.

November

* Sun Hill is evacuated when an unattended holdall is discovered. The Bomb Disposal

Unit is called and Conway announces that the incendiary bomb has been defused. But the holdall erupts in flames and injures Farmer, the Area Traffic Officer. Later they hear that Farmer may lose his sight.

* Brind impersonates a missing girl for a reconstruction of her last movements. The film is shown on the local TV news and the public is questioned.

* Roach's transvestite snout, Roxanne, helps to uncover a child sex "rent boy" business.

December

* A major siege occurs after a man shoots at two bailiffs from a top floor flat. The road is cordoned off, Conway acts as negotiator, the Firearms Unit arrives, followed by the Technical Support Unit, ambulance, fire brigade and canteen van. They learn that the gunman is Polish and an interpreter is sent for. Then they discover he's deaf. He is eventually found crouched under a table.

* A car containing the body of a dead girl is pulled from the river. The owner says that he lent it to a friend - Cryer's son, Patrick - who is charged with causing death by dangerous driving.

* On hearing that Roach and Frazer are having an affair, Conway warns Roach that it must end or he will be transferred to another Division.

1989

January

* Roach goes to court with Cryer's son Patrick. Sgt. Cryer is followed by Bobby Richards - a girl he found left in a telephone box as a baby and whom the hospital named after him. Bobby wants to find her real mother but Cryer, stunned to hear that Patrick's case was thrown out on a technicality, sends her away. He later sees her photograph on a 'missing' poster.

* DS Greig arrives to join the CID, playing his clarinet.

* Haynes goes undercover for a South London division on the trail of Tubbs and Silver, who are backed by the Yardies and suspected of the murder of a club owner.

February

* Ramsey, on patrol with Melvin, drives the car into a group of children 'for a bit of sport', throws his stick at a tin can on a wall and breaks a window.

* Smith is accused of making a racist remark to a schoolgirl but denies it and confronts Ramsey, claiming that it was he who said it. He knees Ramsey in the groin.

* Burnside goes to a pub in response to a phone call mentioning gold bullion. Nancy Norton, the wife of a prisoner, exchanges words and leaves a carrier bag with him containing two thousand pounds. Burnside is then arrested by Starling and interviewed by Ch. Supt. Pearson - an old adversary - in connection with a corruption enquiry. The money is alleged to be payment for influencing Norton's parole application. Burnside escapes to ring Lines and tell him to bring Nancy in. She identifies Starling as the man who had told her that her husband's parole would be refused unless she helped to frame Burnside.

* Stamp is carpeted for his poor driving record - ten accidents, £16,000 worth of damage and a replacement post box.

March

* Smith goes undercover as a soccer hooligan and tips the station off about a gang fight. Some of the gang are arrested but others escape and go after Smith. He is slashed on

the arm with a knife and has to run for his life.

* Melvin stumbles on a gang of arms dealers whilst investigating a report of suspicious activity in an old warehouse. He is knocked unconscious, gagged and handcuffed but eventually discovered.

* Dashwood reports Burnside to Conway when he sees him making a suspicious telephone call after a raid briefing. Part of a gang of pornographers escapes in the raid. Suspicion falls on Burnside, although he is innocent. He vows to find out who grassed on him.

April

* Martella visits a young black prisoner who says that he wants her to visit regularly and bring him drugs. When she refuses he holds her hostage with a knife at her throat.

* Chasing an armed robber, Martella is shot at and her face is bruised and cut. The thief is later caught and Martella is told she will receive a commendation for her part in his capture.

* Greig, Roach and Carver go undercover in a hotel to catch an illegal arms dealer. The job goes wrong when an innocent woman is blown up recovering a stolen car planted and booby trapped by one of the dealer's enemies.

May

* Impressed by a Stress Counselling Course he's attended, Conway puts up notices inviting staff to discuss their personal problems with him. But they are suspicious of his motives and resent the intrusion into their privacy.

* An influx of prisoners, displaced by a Prison Officers' dispute, causes over-crowding, health hazards and a strain on manpower at Sun Hill.

* Roach is accused of attempted murder when a teenager he is chasing falls off a roof. The boy's friend, who made the accusation, later

admits he lied. The teenager dies of his injuries.

June

* Smith encounters a lorry jack-knifed across the road with a crushed car underneath. Assistance is delayed by traffic. The car's occupants are dead but the lorry driver is unharmed and he blames a parked van and the speed of the car. The van owner accuses him of reading a newspaper at the wheel. With no back-up Smith loses control of the situation. After admitting that he was unable to cope Smith tells Martella that he is leaving the force.

* A Falklands veteran threatens to detonate a bomb in a busy shopping centre unless his dead companions are returned to England. Edwards and Ramsey find a rocket launcher in the Gents, which is safely defused.

* Brownlow welcomes WPC Marshall, replacing Hollis as the new Local Intelligence Officer.

July

* Mrs Lines, Tosh's wife, causes a disturbance at a bank and embarrasses Smith and Edwards who are sent to deal with the situation. Lines is sent to sort his wife out. Before he arrives the bank is raided by armed robbers. All inside are held hostage. Over a phone, left off the hook by Edwards, Penny learns of the raid and sends all units to the area. Ramsey is shot trying to stop Lines from entering the bank and rescuing his wife and children.

* Ackland and Melvin travel to Cumbria to collect a prisoner wanted for a public order offence. Two men overpower Melvin and Ackland when they stop to freshen up and rescue the prisoner who turns out to be an international terrorist.

* Cryer is viciously attacked when he visits a disqualified driver suspected of seriously injuring a 9-year-old girl in a hit and run.

August

* Frazer questions Penny's choice of Martella for domestic violence duties.
* Roach arrives at Hendon for an interview with the Inspector's Promotion Board. It is re-scheduled for the afternoon so he and another applicant go to the pub for lunch and get involved in a brawl with another customer. Roach gets head-butted and cannot staunch the flow of blood. At his interview the Board ask about the punch-up and Roach sees his chance of promotion rapidly fading.

* Roach fails the promotion board. Burnside commiserates and admits that he has no chance of promotion whilst Brownlow is in charge. But he persuades him to delay resigning.
* PC Smith is suprised by a Kissogram, in the form of Brind, on his last day at Sun Hill.

September

* Brind welcomes the newest recruit - Asian WPC Norika Datta.
* Stamp responds to an harassment complaint from an attractive girl in her late twenties, wearing an open shirt over a bikini. He has to fight off both her sexual advances and the fire she starts after his rejection.
* Hollis and Stamp, visiting a school fete, volunteer to be clamped in the stocks and are soaked with water by an 11-year-old and his gang.

October

* Brind is asked out by a customer in a pub. She refuses but is embarrassed when, back at Sun Hill, she learns that he is Special Branch Inspector Ray McCann.
* Frazer attends a training centre where she has to deal with a mock riot. She fails to control her team and the instructor says he must report her failure to her superior.
* With the help of Conway and Burnside, McCann apprehends international fugitive Tony Grimes, wanted in connection with supplying prostitutes to foreign diplomats and the murder of one of the hookers. As the Special Branch cars leave Sun Hill they are fired on. Grimes is killed and McCann wounded.

November

* Sun Hill station has an Open Day and the snooker cup is stolen.
* Burnside spots an intruder at an industrial plant and gives chase. He is knocked unconscious by Simpson, a security guard, who says that he did not realise he was a policeman. However, it is later revealed that the guard is actually a man called Tate, previously arrested by Burnside for robbery, who hit him in revenge.

* Edwards decides to transfer after visiting the Met. Welfare/Counsellor who coaxes him into admitting that it's not only his wife who wants to return to Wales.

December

* Frazer comes up for appraisal with Brownlow and, with her position on the line, she outlines her frustrations as a female officer. Speaking freely she indentifies her stumbling block to promotion at Sun Hill as Conway. Faced with a 'him or me' argument Brownlow won't recommend her for promotion. Frazer tells Burnside she'll re-consider her future.
* PC Quinnan arrives at Sun Hill and teases Turnham about an incident when they were both at Bow St.
* Frazer applies for a course at Bramshill.

1990

January

* Frazer stops Turnham assisting Datta and Ford at a pub disturbance, saying that the women can manage by themselves. But when a fight breaks out the male assistance they need eventually arrives. Later, Brownlow, up-front, agrees with Frazer's feminist views of women policing in 'men's' situations but instructs the Sergeants, via Conway, to countermand any such future instructions of hers.
* A German police officer arrives at Sun Hill on the trail of stolen car engines. The officer is blonde, female and very attractive.
* Frazer and Edwards are leaving Sun Hill. Frazer is going to Bramshill to write a thesis on Women's Career Patterns in the Force. She denies that she's given in and is getting away from the pressures of police life. Brownlow's speech at her reception goes down like a lead balloon. Peters and Penny discuss Frazer's replacement, Insp. Monroe. Meanwhile, Edwards feels he doesn't exist. Brownlow calls him in for a chat but is uncertain who he is and Conway thinks he's already gone. On his way to the pub where his colleagues are holding his leaving party, Edwards hesitates at the door, changes his mind, and walks home.

February

* A van full of teenagers, arrested during a raid on an acid house party, arrive at the station. Amongst them is Susan Peterfield, suspected of drug dealing but confident she won't be charged. Roach discovers why. Her dad is a Commander in the Met. Commander Peterfield is furious when his friend Brownlow refuses to intervene on his daughter's behalf and have her released without charge.
* Quinnan is reprimanded by Monroe for selling calculators to other officers. The crime figures Monroe asked Marshall to compile for Brownlow were distorted because the calculator she bought from Quinnan was duff.
* Cryer and Conway go into training for the Divisional Quarter Marathon.

March

* Martella feels desk bound in her new role as WDC in the CID office. When Lines does her a favour and lets her pick up a prostitute and drug addict he needs as a witness, Martella finds more than she bargained for. The chase turns into a nightmare and her new outfit tears and splits. On her return CID make fun of her bedraggled appearance until she loses her temper with Burnside, and gains acceptance - 'Welcome to the firm, Viv'.
* A Fraud Squad officer arrives to recruit a DS or DC for a special job. Burnside manipulates Lines into the job. Lines rejects it after talking to his wife. It would mean six

months away from his family investigating sectarian corruption in Northern Ireland. Burnside knew this would happen. He wanted to keep his team intact.

* Investigating a reported intruder at a school, Garfield and Quinnan are trapped by a vigilante with a vicious dog.

April

* Brownlow is invited to a Commander's Strategic Planning Meeting and learns that Sun Hill is to be transformed into a station for the 21st century. Normal routine will continue during the refurbishment.
* An officer from MI 11 arrives and asks questions about Turnham, following his application to join Special Branch. Quinnan spills the beans about Turnham's affair with the Chief Super's wife at Bow St. where they both worked, but he is eventually accepted and leaves Sun Hill.
* When refurbishment takes longer than expected Sun Hill has to share facilities with Barton St.
* Brownlow calls in DI Wray from the Drugs Squad for a drugs raid. Burnside resents the 'intrusion'. When a plastic bag of 'cocaine' turns out to be talcum powder, Burnside is suspected of warning the supplier of the operation. He is later cleared and thinks he will soon be rid of Wray but discovers that he is coming to Sun Hill as his new boss.

May

* Alone with Datta, Carver tentatively asks her out, but she is not interested.
* Marshall wants to give up the Collator's job and return to the beat. Cryer asks Monroe who reluctantly agrees to the request.
* Out on the beat Melvin and Quinnan stop a Jaguar dangerously driven by Wilkes. A vehicle check reveals it is stolen and Melvin drives the car back to the station.

Colin Blumenau and Robert Hudson returned to the series as 'Taffy' Edwards and 'Yorkie' Smith for the funeral of PC Ken Melvin.

Instructed by Brownlow to re-park the Jaguar properly, Melvin is blown up by a bomb previously planted in the car. Others, including Brownlow, are slightly injured by the blast. Ambulance and fire crews arrive and Melvin is taken to hospital where he later dies. Wilkes denies he is a member of a terrorist organisation watching Colonel Benson, the owner of the car.
* Every available officer turns out for Melvin's funeral. Burnside even has CID working on a minor case so that they can make it to the service. Stamp reads the lesson.
* Sun Hill, newly refurbished at a cost of £1.3 million, is officially opened and Brownlow

shows a group of VIPs around - including sarcastic local MP, Donovan.

June

* Wray arrives for his first day at Sun Hill and discusses his plans with Brownlow who is pleased at what he hears. But Burnside realises that he and Wray are poles apart in policy and prepares for the coming fight.
* Sun Hill's failure to catch the murderer of children Graeme and Jenny is criticised in the local press.
* Burnside clashes with a team of detectives

from Sheffield down to catch a gang of villains operating up north but based in the Sun Hill manor.

July

* Mickey Smart, a known villain, is arrested by Burnside for a restaurant robbery. Smart makes a run for it and emerges on a rooftop. His wife informs Burnside that he is in ill health and has recently been released from hospital after jumping from a bedroom window. Cryer climbs up, unseen, whilst Burnside tries to reassure him that he will not go to prison but to hospital for treat-

ment. Cryer tries to grab Smart but is too late and he jumps.

* Quinnan visits a local school and notices a man with a large soft toy dog dressed in red, talking to a group of children. His name is Donald Blake and he is talking about 'dogs in danger'. Quinnan remembers a wino's description of 'a big dog in a red coat driving a car' during an enquiry about the murder of Graeme and Jenny. Roach scoffs that the man was drunk, but Blake later confesses all to Penny, including further unsolved child murders in Bristol. Quinnan is recommended for a commendation.

* Roach eavesdrops on Wray and Ackland and tells Burnside that they may be having an affair. Rumours are soon rife.

WPC Ackland (Trudie Godwin) and DCI Gordon Wray (Clive Wood). Is there romance in the air?

August

* Loxton is reprimanded for victimising Young after losing to him at cards. Cryer also warns him about his attitude in general.

* Staff feel that Monroe has overstepped the mark when he searches through their lockers for a jemmy that has gone missing from the property store.

* Quinnan annoys Monroe by arriving at the station wearing a personal stereo. Monroe

decides it's time for Quinnan's appraisal and goes gunning for him. Miraculously, Quinnan manages to stay out of trouble.

September

* Cryer is teased for being a beneficiary in the will of Tilly Lane, an ex-prostitute.

* A man makes a complaint of intimidation against Loxton, and the new Community Liason Officer, Langham, tells Conway that he has heard other such accusations. Conway asks Penny to keep an eye on him.

* Brownlow officially opens Sun Hill's first mobile Crime Prevention Centre. Datta and the Crime Prevention Officer later leave the caravan locked up in a car park and it is stolen.

October

* WPC French, the new black recruit, arrives and on her first patrol with Peters collars a clothing thief named Redpath, who runs into her whilst being pursued by Roach, Carver and Lines. Earlier, a flustered French had been 'serenaded' by a group of workmen outside a coffee stall and threatened to arrest them unless they stopped. The CID officers, hiding in a van waiting for Redpath, secretly filmed the proceedings on a video camera which an amused Lines planned to show in the pub later as part of his birthday celebrations. However, French manages to swap the tape for an old surveillance one of Lines chatting up prostitutes on the manor.

* Wray asks Ackland out for a drink. In the pub she tells him he is premature in suggesting they spend a night together. Dinner is all she'll agree to.

* Chasing armed robbers, Stamp is shot and Cryer shoots the robber, Harris, who turns his shotgun on him. It later transpires that Harris could not have fired at Cryer because he was out of ammunition. In light of the

inevitable enquiry, Brownlow advises Cryer to take some time off.

November

* Dining out with his girlfriend, Roach ejects a drunk who is causing trouble and holds him until the police arrive and take him to Sun Hill. However, Penny will not accept a prisoner without an arresting officer and tells Garfield and Stamp to call Roach in. But he has left the restaurant. An angry Monroe demands that Roach be found. He refuses to come to the station saying that he is off duty and it is not his arrest. Eventually Peters collects him and Monroe records an official caution in Roach's pocket book for Dereliction of Duty.
* Tony Jarvis is released from jail and Roach suspects he will want revenge on his wife, Kim, who shopped him and filed for divorce. Roach has an added interest because he has been having an affair with Kim. He tails Jarvis to her house and suspects a parcel left

on her doorstep to be a bomb. Monroe is alerted, officers clear nearby flats, a fire engine arrives along with the bomb squad and local press. To his embarrassment the parcel contains money and a letter saying that he doesn't bear a grudge and to use some of the cash to buy Roach a drink.
* Cryer feels he's a political liability due to the adverse publicity surrounding his shooting of an "unarmed" man. Brownlow believes it might be better if he were transferred but Conway and Monroe disagree and Cryer stays.

December

* Cryer is presented with an inscribed statue of a Victorian sergeant by his colleagues to mark his twenty years in the Force. Leaving the pub, Penny is stopped in his car by two

policemen from Barton St. He is charged with drink/driving, despite claiming that he has been framed in retaliation for reporting a Barton St officer (Coles) for assaulting a prisoner. Faced with losing his job, Penny decides his best course is to resign on medical grounds - claiming that he is still suffering from an old gunshot injury.

* Wray is transferred because of his affair with Ackland, after his wife informs their new DAC, Hicks.
* On her way to Sun Hill, new DCI, Kim Reid, stops for a sandwich, overhears a man trying to con money out of a pair of tourists and arrests him. CID discuss her classy arrival - with a prisoner and a packet of sandwiches.

1991

January

* Loxton is formally suspended from driving police vehicles pending an enquiry, after colliding with another car during a chase.

Course. Despite some criticism from DAC Hicks, who has recently joined the board, the interview goes well.
* Dashwood's transfer request to the Fraud Squad is turned down.

* A gang of villains brutally attack Roach in a pub and knock him senseless. Maitland arrives and with a lightning kick to the ringleader's groin, sends him down. The others surrender.
* Marshall stops two youths and she is attacked and indecently assaulted. Monroe later arrests her attacker.

February

* Brownlow goes to Scotland Yard for an Interview Board in connection with his application to attend the Senior Command

* Dashwood is forced onto a roof at gunpoint and made to wave to the police below by a villain named Bailey. Armed police climb the stairs and hear a shot. On the roof they find Dashwood unhurt and that Bailey has shot himself.

March

* Burnside agrees to let Roach work solo on a security van robbery despite Reid's insistance that they operate as a team. She reprimands Burnside but Roach indentifies the robber as a man named Heslop. Burnside and Reid arrive at his house to find a handcuffed Heslop being led out by Roach.
* Martella endangers her career and is reprimanded for deliberately reading out inadmissable evidence - a prisoner's previous record - from her notebook in court to try to ensure a conviction.
* French disappears after investigating an incident with a screaming woman in a flat. She is first on the scene at a cot death. Cryer finds her sitting on a park bench recovering from the trauma.

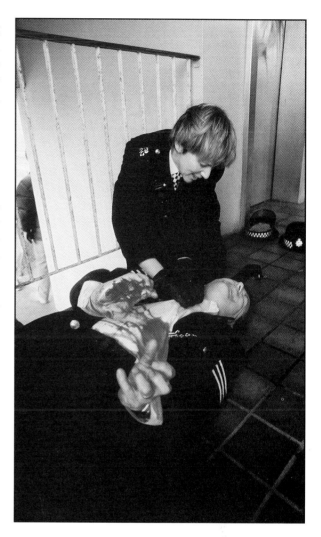

April

* CID place bets on who is going to be made Duty Sgt. The contenders are Cryer and Peters. When Peters turns the job down Cryer accepts it.
* Members of the Serious Crime Squad descend on Sun Hill to investigate how Lennie Powell, a 'supergrass', was shot dead in their custody. Burnside was responsible for stepping down extra cover on Powell after a bogus attempt was made on his life. When Roach refuses to share the blame the two have a bust up.
* Stringer is pushed off a 100ft high ledge in a derelict power station whilst chasing a suspect but grabs some hanging netting to save himself. He was unaware that the suspect had just stabbed Peters.

May

* Ackland takes out a private prosecution against Everton Warwick for assaulting her, after the Crown Prosecution refuses to act. The jury later find him not guilty.
* Dashwood's former nark, Harry Hayes, is arrested for burglary and wants Dashwood to get him off. When he refuses, Hayes claims that Dashwood threatened him and also took money off him. Brownlow contacts the Complaints Investigation Bureau who grill Dashwood over the allegations.
* Lines spots a "ghost" on a bus. He had arrested the man for fraud five years earlier but the man had committed suicide. Burnside is concerned that Lines needs some time off when Lines insists on investigating. It transpires that the original suicide

was faked but before the culprit can be apprehended he effects a genuine suicide.

June

* Lines and Carver are tipped off that the Wilson Boys - a Christian rock band - are carrying drugs. They search them in their dressing room where newspapermen are present and the story hits the front pages when they are arrested for being in possesion of two suspicious-looking packets. The contents turn out to be a mixture of curry powder and mud. Lines is sure that it has all been a publicity stunt set up by their manager, but is unable to prove it.
* Loxton has some explaining to do when blood is found on his truncheon after a street fight in which a man dies.
* Reid is embittered when Brownlow puts

down her new scheme to combat street crime and then presents it to the area hierarchy as a plan he has instructed the Sun Hill Management Team to whip into shape.

July

* Hollis runs into an armed building society robber who grabs him and takes him hostage in a cold store along with a shop assistant. All units are alerted. He is persuaded to release the girl but there is a struggle between the two men, the gun goes off but neither is hurt, and Hollis manages to overpower him.
* Stamp and Hollis discover human skeletons in a flat. Hollis thinks he has uncovered a multiple murder but the bones turn out to have been bought in the Phillipines and imported for sale to medical students.

The Bill Series Index

The Bill

Title   BLUE FOR A BOY
Writer   John Foster
Director   Paul Harrison
Transmission date   6.10.88

Title   CHASING THE DRAGON
Writer   Brendan J Cassin
Director   Frank Smith
Transmission date   11.10.88

Title   THE COOP
Writer   Garry Lyons
Director   Graham Theakston
Transmission date   13.10.88

Title   THE QUICK AND THE DEAD
Writer   Christopher Russell
Director   Philip Casson
Transmission date   18.10.88

Title   WITNESS
Writer   Christopher Russell
Director   Graham Theakston
Transmission date   20.10.88

Title   HERE WE GO LOOPY LOU
Writer   Julian Jones
Director   Brian Farnham
Transmission date   25.10.88

Title   STOP AND SEARCH
Writer   Geoff McQueen
Director   Terry Marcel
Transmission date   27.10.88

Title   SPOOK STUFF
Writer   Geoff McQueen
Director   Terry Marcel
Transmission date   1.11.88

Title   EVACUATION
Writer   Edwin Pearce
Director   Terry Green
Transmission date   3.11.88

Title   PERSONAL IMPORTS
Writer   Kevin Clarke
Director   Brian Farnham
Transmission date   8.11.88

Title   PAPER CHASE
Writer   Barry Appleton
Director   Niall Leonard
Transmission date   10.11.88

Title   INTRUDER
Writer   Roger Parkes
Director   Graham Theakston
Transmission date   15.11.88

Title   CONFLICT
Writer   Al Hunter
Director   Graham Theakston
Transmission date   17.11.88

Title   DUPLICATES
Writer   Simon Moss
Director   Niall Leonard
Transmission date   22.11.88

Title   SNOUT
Writer   Arthur McKenzie
Director   Paul Harrison
Transmission date   24.11.88

Title   OLD HABITS
Writer   Nicholas McInerny
Director   Barry Davis
Transmission date   29.11.88

Title   THE SILENT GUN
Writer   Christopher Russell
Director   Terry Marcel
Transmission date   1.12.88

Title   AN OLD-FASHIONED TERM
Writer   Geoff McQueen
Director   Philip Casson
Transmission date   6.12.88

Title   GETTING STRESSED
Writer   Christopher Russell
Director   Philip Casson
Transmission date   8.12.88

Title   TIGERS
Writer   Edwin Pearce
Director   Terry Marcel
Transmission date   13.12.88

Title   GUESSING GAME
Writer   Peter J Hammond
Director   Jan Sargent
Transmission date   15.12.88

Title   THE ASSASSINS
Writer   Douglas Watkinson
Director   Terry Daw
Transmission date   20.12.88

Title   OUTMODED
Writer   Barry Appleton
Director   Terry Green
Transmission date   22.12.88

Title   DIGGING UP THE PAST
Writer   Barry Appleton
Director   Barry Davis
Transmission date   27.12.88

Title   TAKEN INTO CONSIDERATION
Writer   Lawrence Gray
Director   Chris Hodson
Transmission date   29.12.88

Title   GETTING IT RIGHT
Writer   Barry Appleton
Director   Terry Daw
Transmission date   3.1.89

Title   A REFLECTION OF GLORY
Writer   Brendan J Cassin
Director   Chris Hodson
Transmission date   5.1.89

Title   ONE TO ONE
Writer   Christopher Russell
Director   Jan Sargent
Transmission date   10.1.89

Title   THE MUGGING AND THE GYPSIES
Writer   David Halliwell
Director   Barry Davis
Transmission date   12.1.89

Title   THE CHAIN OF COMMAND
Writer   Christopher Short
Director   Robert Tronson
Transmission date   17.1.89

Title   LIFE AND DEATH
Writer   Kieran Prendiville
Director   Robert Tronson
Transmission date   19.1.89

Title   HOTHEAD
Writer   Edwin Pearce
Director   Philip Casson
Transmission date   24.1.89

Title   STEAMERS
Writer   Gerry Huxham
Director   Terry Green
Transmission date   26.1.89

Title   DUTY ELSEWHERE
Writer   Brendan J Cassin
Director   Jeremy Summers
Transmission date   31.1.89

Title   SATURDAY BLUES
Writer   David Squire
Director   Jeremy Summers
Transmission date   2.2.89

Title   N.F.A.
Writer   Arthur McKenzie
Director   Keith Washington
Transmission date   7.2.89

Title   THE PRICE YOU PAY
Writer   Kieran Prendiville
Director   Keith Washington
Transmission date   9.2.89

Title   CAUGHT RED HANDED
Writer   Barry Appleton
Director   Derek Lister
Transmission date   9.8.88

Title   COCK UP
Writer   Tony Grounds
Director   Brian Farnham
Transmission date   16.2.89

Title   REPERCUSSIONS
Writer   Tony Grounds
Director   Brian Farnham
Transmission date   21.2.89

Title   A DEATH IN THE FAMILY
Writer   John Foster
Director   Chris Hodson
Transmission date   23.2.89

Title   IN THE FRAME
Writer   Barry Appleton
Director   Barry Davis
Transmission date   28.2.89

Title   A GOOD RESULT
Writer   Christopher Russell
Director   Jeremy Summers
Transmission date   2.3.89

Title   CONSCIENCE
Writer   Barry Appleton
Director   Jeremy Summers
Transmission date   7.3.89

Title   SUNDAY SUNDAY
Writer   Fletcher/LeParmentier
Director   Terry Marcel
Transmission date   9.3.89

Title   CLIMATE
Writer   P J Hammond
Director   Brian Parker
Transmission date   14.3.89

Title   BAD COMPANY
Writer   Brendan J Cassin
Director   Terry Marcel
Transmission date   16.3.89

Title   SUSPICIOUS MINDS
Writer   Kieran Prendiville
Director   Terry Green
Transmission date   21.3.89

Title   INTUITION
Writer   Jonathan Rich
Director   Brian Parker
Transmission date   23.3.89

Title   LOSS
Writer   P J Hammond
Director   Brian Farnham
Transmission date   28.3.89

Title   PROCEDURE
Writer   John Milne
Director   Terry Green
Transmission date   30.3.89

Title   LUCK OF THE DRAW
Writer   Patrick Harkins
Director   Keith Washington
Transmission date   4.4.89

Title   NO STRINGS
Writer   Kevin Clarke
Director   Brian Farnham
Transmission date   6.4.89

Title   FOOLS GOLD
Writer   David Squire
Director   Keith Washington
Transmission date   11.4.89

Title   THE VISIT
Writer   Barry Appleton
Director   Alan Wareing
Transmission date   13.4.89

Title   ONE FOR THE LADIES
Writer   Brendan J Cassin
Director   Terry Green
Transmission date   18.4.89

Title   NO SHELTER
Writer   Julian Jones
Director   Terry Marcel
Transmission date   20.4.89

Title   OUT TO LUNCH
Writer   Julian Jones
Director   Brian Parker
Transmission date   25.4.89

Title   FREE WHEEL
Writer   P J Hammond
Director   Alan Wareing
Transmission date   27.4.89

Title   ONLY A BIT OF THIEVING
Writer   Chris Barlas
Director   Brian Parker
Transmission date   2.5.89

Title   COMMUNICATIONS
Writer   Jonathan Rich
Director   Alan Wareing
Transmission date   4.5.89

Title   SILVER LINING
Writer   Colin Giffin
Director   Mike Dormer
Transmission date   9.5.89

Title   SUFFOCATION JOB
Writer   Peter J Hammond
Director   Brian Farnham
Transmission date   11.5.89

Title   MICKEY WOULD HAVE WANTED IT
Writer   Kieran Prendiville
Director   Brian Farnham
Transmission date   16.5.89

Title   BLOOD TIES
Writer   Chris Barlas
Director   Mike Dormer
Transmission date   18.5.89

Title   YOU'LL BE BACK
Writer   Shirley Cooklin
Director   Richard Standeven
Transmission date   23.5.89

Title   FORT APACHE - SUNHILL
Writer   Barry Appleton
Director   Antonia Bird
Transmission date   25.5.89

Title   WASTE
Writer   Al Hunter
Director   Richard Standeven
Transmission date   30.5.89

Title   THE STRONG SURVIVE
Writer   Brendan J Cassin
Director   Sharon Miller
Transmission date   1.6.89

Title   LOVING CARE
Writer   Al Hunter
Director   Michael Owen Morris
Transmission date   6.6.89

Title   BACK ON THE STREETS
Writer   Simon Moss
Director   Alan Wareing
Transmission date   8.6.89

Title   FAT AC
Writer   Julian Jones
Director   John Bruce
Transmission date   13.6.89

Title   SOMEWHERE BY CHANCE
Writer   Barry Appleton
Director   Terry Marcel
Transmission date   15.6.89

Title   A QUIET LIFE
Writer   Simon Moss
Director   Sharon Miller
Transmission date   20.6.89

Title   TOM TIDDLER'S GROUND
Writer   Peter J Hammond
Director   John Bruce
Transmission date   22.6.89

Title   MAKE MY DAY
Writer   Barry Appleton
Director   Michael Ferguson
Transmission date   27.6.89

Title   PROVOCATION
Writer   Edwin Pearce
Director   Michael Ferguson
Transmission date   29.6.89

Title   OVERSPEND
Writer   Christopher Russell
Director   Terry Marcel
Transmission date   4.7.89

Title   BETWEEN FRIENDS
Writer   Barry Appleton
Director   Barry Davis
Transmission date   6.7.89

Title   TRAFFIC
Writer   Christopher Russell
Director   Bill Brayne
Transmission date   11.7.89

Title   THE SACRED SEAL
Writer   Brendan J Cassin
Director   Michael Owen Morris
Transmission date   13.7.89

Title   SUBSEQUENT VISITS
Writer   Arthur McKenzie
Director   Bill Brayne
Transmission date   18.7.89

Title   USER FRIENDLY
Writer   Barry Appleton
Director   Graham Theakston
Transmission date   20.7.89

Title	SMALL HOURS	Title	UNSOCIAL HOURS	Title	FORGET-ME-NOT	Title	MARKET FORCES
Writer	Kevin Clarke	Writer	J C Wilsher	Writer	Russell Lewis	Writer	Peter Brooks
Director	Mike Vardy	Director	Derek Lister	Director	Frank W Smith	Director	Sarah Pia Anderson
Transmission date	3.5.90	Transmission date	17.7.90	Transmission date	25.9.90	Transmission date	6.12.90

Title	VICTIMS	Title	INTERPRETATIONS	Title	SOMETHING TO	Title	ONE FOR THE ROAD
Writer	Jonathan Rich	Writer	Jonathan Rich		REMEMBER	Writer	Michael Crompton
Director	Derek Lister	Director	Julian Amyes	Writer	Christopher Russell	Director	John Strickland
Transmission date	8.5.90	Transmission date	19.7.90	Director	Laura Sims	Transmission date	11.12.90
				Transmission date	27.9.90		

Title	SOMEBODY'S HUSBAND	Title	ANGLES	Title	OFF THE LEASH	Title	START WITH THE
Writer	Jonathan Rich	Writer	Arthur McKenzie	Writer	Chris Russell		WHISTLE
Director	Derek Lister	Director	Roger Tucker	Director		Writer	J C Wilsher
Transmission date	10.5.90	Transmission date	24.7.90	Transmission date	2.10.90	Director	John Strickland
						Transmission date	13.12.90

Title	CANLEY FIELDS	Title	WATCH MY LIPS	Title	FAMILY TIES	Title	OUT OF THE BLUE
Writer	Christopher Russell	Writer	Julian Amyes	Writer	Martyn Wade	Writer	J C Wilsher
Director	Mike Vardy	Director	Patrick Harkins	Director	Chris Lovett	Director	Moira Armstrong
Transmission date	15.5.90	Transmission date	26.7.90	Transmission date	4.10.90	Transmission date	18.12.90

Title	THE NIGHT WATCH	Title	FEELING BRAVE	Title	OLD FRIENDS	Title	STREET SMART
Writer	J C Wilsher	Writer	John Milne	Writer	Nick Collins	Writer	J C Wilsher
Director	Graham Theakston	Director	Richard Holthouse	Director	Michael Kerrigan	Director	Sarah Pia Anderson
Transmission date	17.5.90	Transmission date	31.7.90	Transmission date	9.10.90	Transmission date	20.12.90

Title	TROJAN HORSE	Title	COME FLY WITH ME	Title	PRIDE AND PREJUDICE	Title	SAFE AS HOUSES
Writer	Pat Dunlop	Writer	Peter Gibbs	Writer	Tim Firth	Writer	Russell Lewis
Director	Graham Theakston	Director	Michael Kerrigan	Director	Laura Sims	Director	Tom Cotter
Transmission date	22.5.90	Transmission date	2.8.90	Transmission date	11.10.90	Transmission date	26.12.90

Title	RITES	Title	ATTITUDES	Title	HOUSEY HOUSEY	Title	FRIENDS AND
Writer	Jonathan Rich	Writer	Arthur McKenzie	Writer	John Chambers		NEIGHBOURS
Director	Derek Lister	Director	Richard Holthouse	Director	Bill Brayne	Writer	Christopher Russell
Transmission date	24.5.90	Transmission date	7.8.90	Transmission date	16.10.90	Director	Mike Dormer
						Transmission date	27.12.90

Title	ANSWERS	Title	ROBBO	Title	CONNELLY'S KIDS	Title	GRIEF
Writer	Peter J Hammond	Writer	Brian Finch	Writer	Michael Cameron	Writer	Arthur McKenzie
Director	Chris Hodson	Director	Chris Lovett	Director	Chris Lovett	Director	Graham Theakston
Transmission date	29.5.90	Transmission date	9.8.90	Transmission date	18.10.90	Transmission date	1.1.91

Title	A FRESH START	Title	GROUND RULES	Title	ONE OF THOSE DAYS	Title	THE CHASE
Writer	Christopher Russell	Writer	Geoff McQueen	Writer	Roger Leach	Writer	Carole Harrison
Director	Derek Lister	Director	Michael Kerrigan	Director	Nick Laughland	Director	Stuart Urban
Transmission date	31.5.90	Transmission date	14.8.90	Transmission date	23.10.90	Transmission date	3.1.90

Title	A CASE TO ANSWER	Title	ONCE A COPPER formerly	Title	JACK-THE-LAD	Title	THE ATTACK
Writer	J C Wilsher		VISIT	Writer	Michael Baker	Writer	Philip Palmer
Director	Stuart Burge	Writer	Robin Mukherjee	Director	Bill Hays	Director	John Black
Transmission date	5.6.90	Director	Frank W Smith	Transmission date	25.10.90	Transmission date	8.1.91
		Transmission date	16.8.90				

Title	LINE UP	Title	VENDETTA	Title	BLUE MURDER	Title	CROWN V COOPER
Writer	Elizabeth-Ann Wheal	Writer	Peter Brooks	Writer	Russell Lewis	Writer	C Smyth
Director	Stuart Burge	Director	Graham Theakston	Director	Stuart Urban	Director	Michael Kerrigan
Transmission date	7.6.90	Transmission date	21.8.90	Transmission date	30.10.90	Transmission date	10.1.91

Title	POLICE POWERS	Title	MY FAVOURITE THINGS	Title	EFFECTIVE PERSUADERS	Title	THE GIRL CAN'T HELP IT
Writer	Julian Jones	Writer	Arthur McKenzie	Writer	J C Wilsher	Writer	Arthur McKenzie
Director	Gordon Flemyng	Director	Roger Tucker	Director	Nick Laughland	Director	John Strickland
Transmission date	12.6.90	Transmission date	23.8.90	Transmission date	1.11.90	Transmission date	15.1.91

Title	ACTION BOOK	Title	WIN SOME LOSE SOME	Title	A SENSE OF DUTY	Title	MACHINES
Writer	Christopher Russell	Writer	Jonathan Rich	Writer	Julian Jones	Writer	Peter J Hammond
Director	Graham Theakston	Director	Jeremy Ancock	Director	Bill Hays	Director	Bob Gabriel
Transmission date	14.6.90	Transmission date	28.8.90	Transmission date	6.11.90	Transmission date	17.1.91

Title	TACTICS	Title	UP THE STEPS	Title	LYING IN WAIT	Title	LOOPHOLE
Writer	Arthur McKenzie	Writer	Carolyn Sally Jones	Writer	Chris Boucher	Writer	Michael Baker
Director	Graham Theakston	Director	Jeremy Ancock	Director	Bill Brayne	Director	John Strickland
Transmission date	19.6.90	Transmission date	30.8.90	Transmission date	8.11.90	Transmission date	22.1.91

Title	SCORES	Title	WHERE'S THERE'S A WILL	Title	PLATO FOR POLICEMEN	Title	BOTTLE
Writer	Peter J Hammond	Writer	Patrick Harkins	Writer	Robin Mukherjee	Writer	Arthur McKenzie
Director	Gordon Flemyng	Director	Garth Tucker	Director	Chris Hodson	Director	Graham Theakston
Transmission date	21.6.90	Transmission date	4.9.90	Transmission date	13.11.90	Transmission date	24.1.91

Title	WITCH HUNT	Title	NEAR THE KNUCKLE	Title	TESTIMONY	Title	SAMARITAN
Writer	Christopher Russell	Writer	Ayshe Raif	Writer	Robin Mukherjee	Writer	Brian Finch
Director	Derek Lister	Director	Nick Hamm	Director	Chris Hodson	Director	John Black
Transmission date	26.6.90	Transmission date	6.9.90	Transmission date	15.11.90	Transmission date	29.1.91

TITLE	CLOSE TO HOME	Title	BODY LANGUAGE	Title	DECISIONS	Title	FEAR OR FAVOUR
Writer	Christopher Russell	Writer	Dick Sharples	Writer	Arthur McKenzie	Writer	Christopher Russell
Director	Nick Laughland	Director	Nick Hamm	Director	Tom Cotter	Director	Mike Dormer
Transmission date	28.6.90	Transmission date	11.9.90	Transmission date	20.11.90	Transmission date	31.1.91

Title	BREAKING POINT	Title	WHEN DID YOU LAST SEE	Title	KNOW YOUR ENEMY	Title	START TO FINISH
Writer	Les Pollard		YOUR FATHER	Writer	Nick Collins	Writer	Graham Ison
Director	Peter Barber-Fleming	Writer	Barry Appleton	Director	Moira Armstrong	Director	Laura Sims
Transmission date	3.7.90	Director	Bob Gabriel	Transmission date	22.11.90	Transmission date	5.2.91
		Transmission date	13.9.90				

Title	JUMPING THE GUN	Title	EYE-WITNESS	Title	LIES	Title	NIGHT AND DAY
Writer	David Hoskins	Writer	Christopher Penfold	Writer	Brendan McDonald	Writer	Russell Lewis
Director	Peter Barber-Fleming	Director	Graham Theakston	Director	Roger Tucker	Director	Michael Owen-Morris
Transmission date	5.7.90	Transmission date	18.9.90	Transmission date	27.11.90	Transmission date	7.2.91

Title	WHAT KIND OF MAN?	Title	SUFFICIENT EVIDENCE	Title	OLD WOUNDS	Title	FAVOURS
Writer	Christopher Russell	Writer	Rib Davis	Writer	Ian Briggs	Writer	Martyn Wade
Director	Chris Lovett	Director	Garth Tucker	Director	Roger Tucker	Director	Bob Blagden
Transmission date	10.7.90	Transmission date	20.9.90	Transmission date	29.11.90	Transmission date	12.2.91

Title	BEAT CRIME			Title	JUST FOR THE MOMENT	
Writer	J C Wilsher			Writer	Susan B Shattock	
Director	Nick Laughland			Director	Tom Cotter	
Transmission date	12.7.90			Transmission date	4.12.90	

Sun Hill Roll Call

Principal cast members in 1991

WPC June Akland	Trudie Godwin
Sgt Matthew Boyden	Tony O'Callaghan
Chief Supt Charles Brownlow	Peter Ellis
DI Frank Burnside	Christopher Ellison
DC (formerly PC) Jim Carver	Mark Wingett
Chief Insp (Ops) Derek Conway	Ben Roberts
Sergeant Bob Cryer	Eric Richard
DC Mike Dashwood	John Iles
PC Norika Datta	Seeta Indrani
WPC Suzanne Ford	Vikki Gee-Dare
WPC Delia French	Natasha Williams
PC George Garfield	Huw Higginson
DS Alistair Greig	Andrew Mackintosh
PC Reg Hollis	Jeff Stewart
DC Alfred 'Tosh' Lines	Kevin Lloyd
PC Steven Loxton	Tom Butcher
Sgt John Maitland	Sam Miller
WPC Cathy Marshall	Lynne Miller
WDC (formerly WPC) Viv Martella	Nula Conwell
Insp Andrew Monroe	Colin Tarrant
Sgt Alec Peters	Larry Dann
PC Dave Quinnan	Andrew Paul
DCI Kim Reid	Carolyn Pickles
DS Ted Roach	Tony Scannell
PC Ron Smollett	Nick Stringer
PC Tony Stamp	Graham Cole
PC Barry Stringer	Jonathan Dow
PC Phil Young	Colin Alldridge

Previous principal cast members

PC Timothy Able	Mark Haddigan
WPC Claire Brind	Kelly Lawrence
PC Francis ('Taffy') Edwards	Colin Blumenau
PC Robin Frank	Ashley Gunstock
Insp Christine Frazer	Barbara Thorn
PC Malcolm Haynes	Eamonn Walker
DI Roy Galloway	John Salthouse
Insp Kite	Simon Slater
PC Dave Litten	Gary Olsen
PC Abe Lyttleton	Ronnie Cush
PC Ken Melvin	Mark Powley
PC Pete Muswell	Ralph Brown
PC Patel	Sonesh Sira
Sgt Tom Penny	Roger Leach
PC Pete Ramsey	Nick Reding
PC Nick Shaw	Chris Walker
PC Tony ('Yorkie') Smith	Robert Hudson
PC Richard Turnham	Chris Humphreys
DCI Gordon Wray	Clive Wood

Executive Producer
Michael Chapman

Producers
Tony Virgo
Peter Wolfes

Former Executive Producers
Peter Cregeen
Lloyd Shirley

Former Producers
Richard Bramall
Brenda Ennis
Michael Ferguson
Geraint Morris
Pat Sandys